"If the killer f[...] identify hi[...] rippled thro[...] [...]e."

Her palpable fear [...] [...]s protective instincts into high gear. Ashley was in danger. Her life threatened by what she'd seen. Reining in the urge to comfort and assure her she was safe, Chase let his training prompt him to ask, "Why does Detective Peters think you're involved?"

Her shoulders slumped. "I don't know."

Was he being played? He sent up a quick prayer asking for God's wisdom and guidance here. Keeping his voice from betraying the anxiety her words caused, he said, "We have to get you to the sheriff's station so you can give your statement. You need to be brave now."

For a long moment, she simply stared at him. He could see her inner debate playing out on her face. Trust him or not.

He couldn't help her with the decision.

Finally, she seemed to deflate. "I'm so tired of being scared. I want to be brave."

He covered her icy hand. "I'll help you."

Terri Reed's romance and romantic suspense novels have appeared on the *Publishers Weekly* top twenty-five and Nielsen BookScan top one hundred lists, and have been featured in *USA TODAY*, *Christian Fiction* magazine and *RT Book Reviews*. Her books have been finalists for the Romance Writers of America RITA® Award and the National Readers' Choice Award, and finalists three times for the American Christian Fiction Writers Carol Award. Contact Terri at terrireed.com or PO Box 19555, Portland, OR 97224.

Books by Terri Reed

Love Inspired Suspense

Buried Mountain Secrets
Secret Mountain Hideout

True Blue K-9 Unit

Seeking the Truth

Military K-9 Unit

Tracking Danger
Mission to Protect

Northern Border Patrol

Danger at the Border
Joint Investigation
Murder Under the Mistletoe
Ransom
Identity Unknown

Visit the Author Profile page at Harlequin.com for more titles.

SECRET
MOUNTAIN
HIDEOUT

TERRI REED

HARLEQUIN® LOVE INSPIRED® SUSPENSE

Recycling programs
for this product may
not exist in your area.

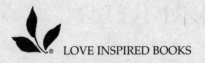

LOVE INSPIRED BOOKS

ISBN-13: 978-1-335-72145-7
ISBN-13: 978-1-335-09054-6 (DTC Edition)

Secret Mountain Hideout

www.Harlequin.com

Printed in U.S.A.

Hear my voice, O God, in my prayer:
preserve my life from fear of the enemy.
Hide me from the secret counsel of the wicked;
from the insurrection of the workers of iniquity.
—Psalm 64:1-2

To the ones I love. May God shine His face upon you always and give you peace.

ONE

It couldn't be.

Ice filled Ashley Willis's veins despite the spring sunshine streaming through the living room windows of the Bristle Township home in Colorado where she rented a bedroom.

Disbelief cemented her feet to the floor, her gaze riveted to the horrific images on the television screen.

Flames shot of out of the two-story building she'd hoped never to see again. Its once bright red awnings were now singed black and the magnificent stained-glass windows depicting the image of an angry bull were no more.

She knew that place intimately.

The same place that haunted her nightmares.

The newscaster's words assaulted her. She grabbed on to the back of the faded floral couch for support.

In a fiery inferno, the posh Burbank restau-

rant, The Matador, was consumed by a raging fire in the wee hours of the morning. Firefighters are working diligently to douse the flames. So far there have been no fatalities, however, there has been one critical injury.

Ashley's heart thumped painfully in her chest, reminding her to breathe. Concern for her friend, Gregor, the man who had safely spirited her away from the Los Angeles area one frightening night a year and a half ago when she'd witnessed her boss, Maksim Sokolov, kill a man, thrummed through her. She had to know what happened. She had to know if Gregor was the one injured.

She had to know if this had anything to do with her.

"Mrs. Marsh," Ashley called out. "Would you mind if I use your cell phone?"

Her landlady, a widow in her mideighties, appeared in the archway between the living room and kitchen. Her hot-pink tracksuit hung on her stooped shoulders but it was her bright smile that always tugged at Ashley's heart. The woman was a spitfire with her blue-gray hair and her kind green eyes behind thick spectacles.

"Of course, dear. It's in my purse." She pointed to the black satchel on the dining room table. "Though you know, as I keep saying, you should get your own cell phone. It's not safe for a young lady to be walking around without any means of calling for help."

They had been over this before. Ashley didn't want anything attached to her name.

Or rather, her assumed identity—Jane Thompson.

Putting the name she was using in some system where it could be flagged and she could be discovered in Bristle Township was a disaster she wanted to avoid at all costs.

So far, using the identification Gregor had given her had worked. She'd been too stunned at the time to question where he'd obtained the driver's license, social security card and credit card, all with the name Jane Thompson. She suspected she wouldn't have liked the answer had she asked. No one so far had questioned that she wasn't Jane Thompson. She didn't know what she'd do if the thin line keeping her safe disappeared and her true identity became known.

A shudder of dread, followed closely by a jab of guilt at deceiving the good people of Bristle Township, made her gut tighten. She prayed God would forgive her for doing what she had to in order to survive.

"I just need to make a quick phone call," Ashley assured her landlady as the urgent drive to know who was injured consumed her.

If she could have bought a burner phone in Bristle Township she would have, but that wasn't an option. First, none of the local stores carried one—she'd discreetly searched—and second, everyone would know about such a purchase the moment she made it.

Thankfully, Mrs. Marsh's data plan included free long distance, as well as Wi-Fi. Mrs. Marsh's children, who both lived in Texas, had sent her the phone so that they could communicate with her.

With phone in hand, Ashley quickly searched for the hospitals in and around the Burbank area. She called each listed and on the fourth try found the hospital where the critically injured victim of The Matador fire had been taken.

Her heart sank to have her fear confirmed that Gregor Kominski, the restaurant's manager, had been the one hurt. Anxiety made her limbs shake beneath the khaki pants and long sleeve T-shirt sporting the Java Bean logo on the front breast pocket and the back. She had been on her way out the door for work when she'd seen the news.

Had the fire been set intentionally? Had Gregor suffered because of her?

"Are you a relative of Mr. Kominski's?" the woman from the hospital on the other end of the line questioned.

Biting her lip, Ashley debated her answer. She didn't want to lie, but she doubted they would give her much information if she admitted she wasn't related to the man. Finally, she hedged, allowing the woman to make her own assumption. "I'm calling from out of town. What can you tell me? Is he going to be okay?"

"He remains in critical condition," the woman said. "Would you like to leave a name and a number for updates?"

Ashley quickly hung up. No, she didn't want to leave a name and number. She didn't want there to be any trace of her reaching out for information. The call had been a risk. One she hoped she wouldn't have to pay for with her life.

Gossip in Bristle Township traveled faster than the wind off the mountain. Ashley couldn't help but overhear several customers of the Java Bean coffee shop talking about a detective from California asking questions about a mysterious woman.

Heart beating in her throat, Ashley spilled milk all over the espresso machine. With shaky hands, she quickly wiped up the mess and finished making the specialty drink.

Just this morning she'd learned of the fire that had destroyed The Matador restaurant and sent her friend to the hospital. Now a police officer from the same state was in town. Coincidence? Or was she on the verge of being discovered?

Ethan Johnson, a local farmer, stared at her from beneath the brim of a well-worn baseball cap as she handed him the steaming cup of mocha cappuccino. "Do you have a sister?"

Her tongue stuck to the roof of her mouth as she mutely shook her head.

"Hmm. I guess we all have a doppelganger," he commented. His blue veined hands cupped the to-go container as if the warmth of the liquid inside was soothing to the arthritis evident in the swollen joints of his fingers.

Forcing herself to speak, she asked, "Why do you say that?"

"You vaguely resemble the woman in the photo the lawman was asking me about," he replied with a shrug. He lifted the cup and blew through the hole on the lid as he walked away.

Though she barely resembled her old self,

terror of being exposed ripped through Ashley. She'd been careful to keep her appearance understated so she could blend in better. Though the dye job she'd done right before landing in Bristle Township hadn't turned out quite the way she'd expected. Much too flashy.

The carton of hair dye had claimed she'd end up with honey blond hair. She touched the short platinum blond strands curling around her face. Sudden sadness and anger at the circumstances that had forced her to change not only her hair color and style but also her whole life swamped her, weighing her down.

One simple distracted moment and her world had spun out of control.

Knowing things could be so much worse— she could be dead—she quickly removed her apron and hurried over to the owner of the Java Bean, Stephen Humphrey. He was a big teddy bear of a man with two teenage kids who helped out on the weekends.

"Hey, boss. I need to take a break, if that's okay. I forgot I promised Mrs. Marsh I would help her with something." Like protecting her from me.

Ashley's insides twisted with guilt. She hated having to keep her true identity a secret from these people who had shown her such kindness.

She knew Stephen had a soft spot for Mrs. Marsh. The whole town did. Mrs. Marsh and her late husband had been beloved grade school teachers. Everyone who had grown up in town had been in her or her late husband's classes. Ashley had heard so many wonderful stories of how Mr. and Mrs. Marsh had made a difference in people's lives.

Just as Mrs. Marsh was making a huge difference in Ashley's life. More guilt and regret heaped on her head, making her scalp tingle. She wanted to scrub the past year and a half away, go back in time and undo what was done. But she couldn't.

The only thing she could do was run to stay alive.

"Sure," Stephen replied. "Just be back for the afternoon rush."

She smiled tightly but refrained from promising. It was time for her to leave Bristle Township as soon as possible. The thought pinched, creating a pang of sorrow. She liked the town and her job. She'd started to make friends, letting people into her heart. Foolish on her part.

Over the last year she'd saved up so she could afford to move on. She'd only stopped in the small mountainside community and taken the job at the coffee shop because she'd run out of the money Gregor had given her. He'd told her never to contact him again and she hadn't wanted to put her mother in danger by contacting her.

Not that Irene Willis would have been in any position to help her only child, nor would she have made much effort if she could. Irene barely made a living waiting tables at a truck stop outside Barstow, California, and Ashley was positive her mom's life was less complicated without her daughter to set off her temper. One of the many reasons Ashley had left as quickly as she could when she turned eighteen.

Ashley's only option had been staying in one place long enough to earn more money to keep running for her life. She hadn't meant to stay so long. But life had become comfortable and she'd believed herself secure in this quaint mountain hamlet. Maybe if she'd stayed in Barstow or chosen a different path, she wouldn't be here now.

An illusion of safety had kept her here. Another mistake she couldn't afford. And now she was on the brink of being found out. She had no doubt that the detective was hunting for her. She couldn't let him succeed in tracking her down.

She hurried out the back entrance of the Java Bean, taking a deep breath of the pine-scented air. She crossed the town park, trying to keep a low profile. The park was filled with moms and their children too young for school. A few elderly couples strolled along the street. A horn honked, startling Ashley. She glanced around, fear slithering through her, making her muscles tense. Two cars vied for the same parking space in front of the bookstore on the main street. Breathing a little easier she hurried on, cutting through the library parking lot, and walked fast down the residential street leading to Mrs. Marsh's place.

The trees along the sidewalk were beginning to blossom. Soft pink petals floated to the ground on a slight breeze. Ashley barely noticed the beauty today, her mind tormented with anxiety.

Managing to reach the boarding house without being seen, she gathered her meager belongings, left an apologetic note and some cash for Mrs. Marsh. Then putting up the hood of her navy down jacket to cover her bright hair, she retraced the same path she'd taken earlier and made her way to the Bristle

Hotel where the interstate bus picked up and dropped off passengers.

A teenager on a bike rode by, waving at her. She had no choice but to wave back to Brady Gallo. Maybe he wouldn't mention to his older sister that he'd seen Jane. It pained Ashley to leave Maya, Leslie and Kaitlyn—the three women who'd befriended her—without a goodbye, but it couldn't be helped.

At the Bristle Hotel, a beautiful old building that dated back to the township's conception, Ashley checked with the front desk clerk and learned a bus was due to arrive within minutes and was headed to Montana. She bought a ticket and then took a position behind a pillar on the wide porch to wait for the bus. There were a couple of other people waiting and she purposely ignored them. The last thing she needed was to engage in idle conversation.

She hoped and prayed she made it out of town before she was found or stopped.

The bus rolled in and she hurried to stow her bag in the undercarriage compartment, then moved to wait at the door behind a guy who needed a shower. The stench coming from his unwashed hair made her eyes water. He'd probably been hiking on the popular trails that began right on the edge of Bristle and threaded up into the mountains.

She hung back as long as she dared, allowing space between them. There were already several people onboard the bus. Seemed Montana was the destination of choice today.

The guy in front of her showed his ticket to the driver and boarded.

"Jane! Wait."

Hesitating, Ashley warily turned to find Deputy Chase Fredrick striding toward her, undeniably handsome in his brown uniform. His sandy blond hair swept over his forehead in an appealing way and his intense blue eyes bored into her. He'd always been kind and charming when he'd come into the Java Bean for coffee.

In different circumstances, she might have been tempted to flirt with him, but there was no place in her life for a man. It was bad enough she'd made friends who were going to be hurt and disappointed by her departure. She regretted causing anyone pain and wouldn't make that mistake again.

What did the deputy want? Dread clawed through her. Was her ruse up? Would she find herself in jail? Or worse—dead?

Desperate to get on the bus, Ashley thrust

her ticket at the driver, but he didn't reach for it as he stared at her a moment and then turned his gaze to the deputy who'd come to a halt at her side and touched her elbow.

Panic revved Ashley's pulse. "What are you doing here?"

"I could ask you the same thing." His blue gaze searched her face. "Why are you leaving town?"

Stiffening her spine, she replied, "It's none of your business."

"It is my business if you're a criminal," he stated in a low voice.

She drew back. Fear fluttered in her chest. "I don't know what you're talking about."

Turning to the bus driver, Chase said, "She won't be taking this bus. Can you unload her bags?"

Giving Ashley a cautious glance, the driver's head bobbed. "Straight away, Officer."

"No! I have to go," she protested. "I need to get on this bus."

The driver hurried to the cargo hold and dragged her duffel out, setting it on the ground before resuming his position at the bus door.

Drawing her away from the curious gazes, Chase said, "Jane, be straight with me. There's a detective from Los Angeles here searching for a woman wanted in connection with a murder. And I'm pretty sure the woman in the photo he has is you."

Her stomach dropped. Fear squeezed her lungs, making breathing difficult.

"Did you kill a man?"

She swallowed back the bile rising to burn her throat. "Of course not. I could never—I wouldn't—"

She wasn't a murderer.

But she knew who was.

Gregor had warned her not to tell anyone, not even the police. They were not to be trusted, he'd said. "I've got to go. This is the only bus out today."

"You're not going anywhere—" Chase's voice was hard and his eyes glittered with warning "—until you tell me the truth."

"Last call," the bus driver called out, sliding a cautious glance their way.

Her gaze darted from the bus to Chase. "Please," she pleaded. "I need to leave. You don't understand. If he finds me, he'll kill me."

Confusion tampered down the hardness of Chase's features. "Jane, trust me. I can protect you. Just tell me what it is you're running from."

She shook her head and took a step back.

"No. I was warned not to say anything. Not even to the police. I can't trust you. I can't trust anyone."

The driver stepped into the bus and closed the door. The bus's engine rumbled and a few seconds later a plume of exhaust filled the air as the bus drove away. Frustration pounded a rapid beat at her temple. Now she was trapped with no way out.

Chase snagged her hand and gently coaxed her fist open. "Jane, listen to me carefully." His voice softened to a smooth tone that seemed to coil inside of her. Her pulse leaped. His touch soothed.

"My job is to protect and serve the citizens of Bristle Township. You are one of its citizens." The intensity in his clear gaze mesmerized her. "I will protect you. If you committed a crime, it is better for you to face it than to run."

Though his hands were warm and reassuring, her heart turned cold. She jerked away from him. "No. I didn't commit a crime. I didn't see anything. I don't know anything."

He stepped closer, invading her space. "I understand you're afraid. Whatever it is, I will be with you the whole way. Please, trust me."

She angled her head to stare at him. "Why is my trust so important to you?"

As if her words were a splash of cold water, he abruptly stepped back. "It's my job to protect you."

She shook her head with a dash of cynicism. "I know you want to believe you can protect me, but the type of people I need protection from don't respect authority. They'd just as soon kill you as look at you."

Chase stood tall as if her words had been a personal assault. "Jane, tell me what you know."

She glanced around to make sure she wouldn't be overheard. She hated how exposed and vulnerable she felt out in the open. She gestured for him to follow her beneath the shade of a large Douglas fir. "If I tell you, will you help me get out of here?"

"If you tell me, I promise I will protect you."

More frustration bubbled inside her. What choice did she have? Her only option was to trust Chase and his promise of protection until she had an opportunity to run again. She had to stay vigilant if she wanted to stay alive.

Her heart raced. Her gaze darted from shadow to shadow, half expecting Maksim Sokolov to step out from behind a tree like a bogeyman from a horror movie. "A year and a half ago—" her voice dipped as the secret she'd held inside escaped like a bat out of a dark cave "—I witnessed a murder."

Jane's words echoed through Chase's brain. Sympathy squeezed his heart. Ever since the detective, who'd appeared this morning without warning at the sheriff station, had shown Chase the photo of a woman with long dark hair and bangs dressed in a black dress and pumps at the back door of a brick building, Chase's stomach had been tied in knots.

Though only the woman's profile had been visible, there had been something vaguely familiar about the curve of her cheek, the line of her jaw. And then it had come to him. The woman in the photo was Jane.

And she apparently was hiding in Bristle Township because she'd witnessed a murder. "Tell me what happened."

She shook her head. "If the killer finds out that I can identify him…" A visible shudder rippled through her. "He will kill me and anyone else in his path."

Her palpable fear sent all his protective instincts into high gear. She was in danger. Her life threatened by what she'd seen. Reining in the urge to comfort and assure her that she was safe, he let his training prompt him to ask, "Why is Detective Peters convinced you're involved?"

She turned to pluck the bark off the tree. Her shoulders slumped. "I don't know."

Was he being played? He sent up a quick prayer, asking for God's wisdom and guidance here. Keeping his voice from betraying the anxiety her words caused, he said, "We have to get you to the sheriff's station so you can give your statement. You need to be brave now."

Chase hoped she would come willingly. He didn't want to have to compel her by putting her in cuffs.

For a long moment, she simply stared at him. He could see her inner debate with herself playing out on her face. Trust him or not.

He couldn't help her with the decision.

Finally, she seemed to deflate. "I'm so tired of being scared. I want to be brave."

He covered her icy hand. "I'll help you."

Snagging her duffel with his free hand, he walked with her away from the hotel. They hadn't gone far when a black SUV pulled up alongside them and Detective William Peters hopped out. The tall, bulky man wore a wrinkled gray suit, white button-down shirt and red tie. His dark hair brushed the edges of his collar.

There was something about the man's gruff demeanor that had rankled Chase from the second they'd met. He chalked it up to city vs. small town. One of the many reasons Chase left the Chicago PD after only a year. He hadn't wanted to become jaded like so many of his fellow officers.

Chase believed in good over evil, that the right side of the law would win in the end. And justice wasn't prejudiced or affected by social status. Maybe that made him naive as some had said. He didn't care. He had faith that he was doing what God wanted for his life.

Detective Peters's dark eyes glittered with triumph. "There you are." He opened the rear passenger door. "Get in. We have a plane to catch."

Jane clutched Chase's arm. She made no move to comply.

"Hold on a minute," Chase told the detective. "We need to do this the right way. We go to the sheriff's station so we can make a proper transfer to your custody."

Peters shook his head. "No way. She's coming with me now. I have a warrant that gives me the right to take her into custody on sight."

Chase didn't recall any mention of a warrant. "The sheriff will want to talk with her."

"There's no time for that." Peters stepped forward and grabbed Jane by the arm, yanking her from Chase's grasp. He pushed her inside the back passenger side of the SUV.

"You can't just take her away," Chase argued. "There's protocol to follow."

Peters got in Chase's face. "Back off. If you have an issue, then call the brass. I've got my orders."

"Chase?"

Jane's anxiety curled through Chase. "I'm going with you. I'll get my own plane ticket. Even if I have to fly on a different airline." He stepped forward to slide into the back seat with Jane when Peters slammed the door shut, blocking Chase from following her into the vehicle.

Peters shoved Chase back a step and glared. "This is my collar, not yours. I'm not letting some Podunk deputy interfere with my investigation."

Taken aback by the man's hostility, Chase put his hand on the butt of his weapon. Drawing on a fellow officer wasn't something he wanted to do, but if the man continued with his aggressive behavior, Chase would have little choice. "She's a witness, not a suspect."

"That's for others with a higher pay grade to decide. She's coming with me." Peters jumped into the vehicle.

Chase grabbed the back door handle but it was locked. He banged on the driver's side window. "You can't just take her like this."

The SUV's engine revved. Peters hit the gas and the SUV peeled away, forcing Chase to jump aside to avoid being hit.

This wasn't right. There was a proper way of doing things. Chase ran to the sheriff's station. At the front desk, he asked Carole if she could get the chief of the Los Angeles Police Department on the line for the sheriff. Then he moved into the inner sanctuary of the station. His voice shook with anger as he told the sheriff and the other deputies about Jane and what had just transpired.

"I've got the Burbank Police Department on the line," Carole called from her desk. "Should I send the call to your desk, Sheriff?"

"No, send it to Chase's," Sheriff Ryder replied.

Stunned, Chase stared. "Sir?"

"You're running point on this one," the sheriff replied.

Not about to question his boss, Chase sat at his desk and punched the blinking light. A second later a man's deep voice came on the line. "Chief Macintosh, how can I help you?"

Chase hurriedly explained the situation, giving his protest at the detective's manhandling of their citizen.

There was a long pause before Chief Macintosh replied, "You say this man had Detective William Peters's identification?"

A strange question. An unsettled apprehension curled through Chase. "He did."

"The man's an imposter," Macintosh said. "Detective William Peters is dead. Murdered during an undercover operation."

TWO

The air swooshed out of Chase's lungs. If he hadn't been sitting, he'd have fallen to the floor. His mind raced and his blood pounded. The man posing as Detective William Peters was a fake. The real detective was dead.

Jane was in danger.

Kidnapped. And Chase had let it happen.

Guilt reached up to throttle his windpipe. He'd made a horrible mistake by not stopping the fake detective. Now Jane would pay the price.

"Whoever this woman is, she could be a potential witness to the real Detective Peters's murder," Chief Macintosh continued.

Chase's stomach sank. "She claims she can ID a killer."

Excitement buzzed in the chief's voice. "Did she give a name?"

"No, sir." She'd been too afraid. He could

only imagine how terrified she was now. She'd tried to warn him not to trust anyone. Chase had lost control of the situation. A rookie mistake. He wasn't a rookie anymore. Self-anger burned in his gut.

"You need to find this phony detective before he kills her," Chief Macintosh said, his tone grim.

"I will." Chase hung up with knots in his stomach.

The man said they had a plane to catch, which meant they were headed to Denver. He needed the state patrol's help. He jerked to his feet. "Carole, can you get the state patrol on the line?"

"Chase?" Deputy Kaitlyn Lanz rose from her desk. "What's wrong?"

"The real Peters is dead. The man posing as him most likely is an assassin sent to silence Jane. We have to find them."

Eyes wide with a mix of worry and surprise, Kaitlyn said, "Yes, of course."

Carole hurried from her desk. "Sheriff, the phones are blowing up again. A speeding black SUV nearly ran down Brady Gallo. Others are reporting the vehicle heading up Bishop Summit."

Chase was familiar with the forestry road on

the backside of Eagle Crest Mountain, which led to the ski resort at the top. It was a dangerous, twisty climb with lots of cliffs on one side. The assassin wasn't taking Jane to Denver but to a remote area to kill her.

"Also, Lucca Chinn is here, wanting to know what's going on," Carole said.

Groaning aloud, Chase jerked his gaze to the sheriff. The last thing they needed was *The Bristle Township Gazette*'s publisher, reporter and custodian—the man was a one-person operation—sticking his nose into the situation. Even a small town had someone who insisted the public needed to be kept informed, and Lucca Chinn had appointed himself the resident news source.

"I'll take care of Chinn," the sheriff stated. "You go."

Galvanized into action, Chase ran out the door with deputies Daniel Rawlings and Kaitlyn Lanz on his heels.

"I'll be right behind you." Kaitlyn peeled away and ran toward her own vehicle.

Chase didn't stop to question why she needed to drive her own truck pulling a horse trailer as he slid into the driver's seat of one of the department-issued vehicles while Daniel hopped into the passenger seat. Chase lifted a prayer that he would get to Jane before it was too late.

Ashley stared out the window of the rear passenger seat of the big black SUV as the vehicle roared up the access road to the ski resort. Green trees and various other plants growing wild along the edges of the road were a blur. The SUV's tires squealed as the vehicle sped through a curve in the road.

"I don't understand," she said to the man in front. "I thought you said we were going to the airport. This isn't the way to Denver."

She could only see his profile at this angle. His nose had a lump on the top like he'd broken it and not had it set well. His dark hair was unruly. Everything about him was at odds with the button-down way Deputy Chase Fredrick presented himself. "Shut up," the detective growled.

Alarm raised the hairs on her arms. She didn't know what this man was up to but the dread squeezing her lungs urged her to escape. She tried the door handle, but the door wouldn't open. He'd activated the vehicle's child locks, keeping her trapped inside. She tried the window, but it too wouldn't open. Not that either option was an escape when the

SUV was buzzing along like a rocket on the twisty road.

She kicked the front seat. "Hey! What are you doing? Where are you taking me?"

He ignored her.

Who was this man driving her up the mountain? Was he really a detective? Fear scraped along her nerves. Had her captor been sent by Maksim Sokolov?

The vehicle made a sharp turn into an overlook gravel turnout and came to an abrupt halt, throwing her forward. The seat belt snapped into a locked position, keeping her from flying into the back of the front seat. The strap cut into her chest. Once the pressure lessened, she rubbed at the place where the seat belt had no doubt left a mark.

The detective climbed out of the SUV and came around to her side of the vehicle. She quickly unbuckled and scooted across to the other side of the back seat as he yanked open the door. She attempted to climb into the front driver's seat but her attacker reached in and grabbed her by the ankles, dragging her toward him.

Frantic, she kicked, hoping to dislodge his grip, but his hands were like manacles, his fingers digging into her flesh and not letting go.

He yanked her out of the SUV, her back bumping painfully on the edge of the door frame. She landed flat on the ground with a jarring jolt. Gravel and grit bit into her through her clothes.

Her assailant loosened his grip for a fraction of a second, which was enough time for her to break out of his grasp with a forceful jerk. She jumped to her feet and ran toward the road, hoping someone else would drive by. Feet pounded behind her. She pushed herself to move faster, but she'd never been a strong runner.

Her captor caught her, grabbing her by the waist and lifting her off her feet. She pummeled his arms and lashed out with her feet.

"You are so dead," he growled. "Even if I hadn't been sent here to kill you, I'd do it just because."

"Please, no. I haven't told anyone what I saw," she beseeched the man, hoping for mercy. "You can tell Mr. Sokolov I won't talk."

Ignoring her pleas, her kidnapper carried her away from the road, past the SUV and dragged her across the lookout barrier. There was an overhang not far below.

"Move it," he demanded, giving her a push, forcing her down the steep incline.

Her tennis shoes made the going rough, as the rubber slipped on the loose dirt and rocks. Using her arms, she tried to keep her balance, fearing that she'd take a header over the side of the cliff.

"But you're a law enforcement officer," she exclaimed, shocked by his words that he truly did intend to kill her. "You can't mean to really harm me. What about your oath to protect?"

He let out an evil laugh that sent chills down her spine. "The police think you're a killer. Besides, no one is going to care when you're dead."

His words sliced her open. "How much did Mr. Sokolov pay you?" she demanded, wishing she could offer him more, but she had no money. "How much is my life worth?"

"Enough to set me up for the rest of my life," he said. "No more talking. Time for you to die."

Terror consumed her. The man hauled her toward the ledge that dropped off to a steep cliff with a deep ravine far below. The nightmare she'd been trapped in was coming to a horrifying end.

At the edge of the outcropping, his rough hands reached for her. Acting instinctively, she dropped to the ground, wrapping her arms around his ankles. If she was going over the cliff, so was he.

Chase's hands gripped and re-gripped the steering wheel as he took the corners at a breakneck speed. Adrenaline pumped through his veins, giving him a lead foot.

"Whoa," Daniel said, bracing his hands on the dashboard as the vehicle careened around a curve on the forestry road on the backside of Eagle Crest Mountain. "It's not going to do Jane any good if we drive off the side of the mountain."

Heeding Daniel's words, Chase eased up a fraction. They had to find Jane. He'd already betrayed her trust by letting her go off with an assassin and failed his repeated vow to protect her. The heavy weight of responsibility descended on his shoulders. He couldn't let her die.

The black SUV came into view and Chase hit the brakes, skidding to a halt in front of the vehicle. There was no sign of Jane or the fake detective.

"Radio the sheriff our location." Chase jumped out of the car and ran to the SUV. A quick peek inside confirmed it was empty. He turned around, desperate to figure out where they'd gone. The ground was marred with foot-steps and drag marks in the gravel.

His stomach clenched with dread as he followed the trail to the guardrail. Peering over the side of the cliff, horror filled his veins. On an outcropping stood Peters with Jane clutching his legs for dear life as he tried to pry her from him. His objective was clear. He was going to throw her over the cliff.

Chase vaulted over the guardrail and drew his weapon. He slipped and slid down the hill. "Stop! Put your hands in the air."

Peters twisted toward Chase with a 9mm Glock fitted with a noise suppressor aimed at him.

Chase dove to the side as bullets whizzed past him, so close the air heated. Staying in motion, he rolled to one knee, sighted down the barrel of his weapon and fired. The loud retort echoed over the mountain and battered against his eardrum.

The bullet hit its mark.

For a moment, the assassin's eyes went wide and his mouth dropped open as red bloomed across his white shirt. Then he stumbled back a step, taking Jane with him. The heel of his shoe dislodged a landslide of loose dirt falling to the bottom of the ravine.

Fear choked Chase. Jane was about to go over the cliff with her assailant. "Let go of him!"

Immediately, she responded to his command and released her hold on Peters's legs, scrambling backward seconds before the man took a nosedive down the side of the cliff, disappearing from sight.

Sending a quick praise to God for Jane's safety and asking forgiveness for taking a life, Chase hurried to Jane's side and gathered her in his arms. She clung to him, her body shaking. Through the ringing in his ears, he heard her racking sobs. Her tears soaked the front of his uniform. Chase's heart beat in his throat. He thought he might be sick.

A landslide of rocks sounding from above jolted through him. He jerked his gaze up to the cliff as he tucked Jane behind him.

Daniel slid down the rocky hill much the way Chase had done. Chase let out a compressed breath of relief.

"Wow," Daniel said as he skidded to a halt. "Clean shot. I saw the whole thing. You good?"

His ears still ringing from discharging his weapon, Chase made out the gist of what Daniel said, though his voice sounded muffled.

Chase nodded as he sucked in air, working to calm his racing pulse. Later, he'd deal with the aftermath of taking a life.

Daniel stepped past Chase and peered over the edge of the cliff. He whistled and turned to stare at Chase. "That's a long way down." He moved away from the ledge. "I better call the sheriff and tell him we need a recovery team. You okay to get her up the hill?"

"We'll manage." Chase helped Jane to her feet. He met her terrified gaze. "Take it slow and steady."

He wrapped an arm around her waist and they made the arduous climb up the incline. They ended up having to crawl on hands and knees to keep their center of gravity low, until they reached the guardrail. Chase lifted Jane over the metal rungs and set her on the gravel of the turnout. Then he climbed over, grateful for the stable ground.

Jane wrapped her arms around her middle; her lips trembled and tears streaked down her face. "Are you okay?"

"I am." His hearing was returning and his heart rate had slowed. "You? Did he hurt you?"

"I'll have some bruises." She stared at him, her eyes wide. "You saved my life."

The wonder in her tone scored him to the quick. "If I had been better at my job, you wouldn't have been in the situation in the first place."

"This is not your fault." There was compassion in her tone. "He was a police officer, too."

Chase shook his head. "No. He was an imposter."

Her eyes widened in shock. She let out a shuddering breath. "If you hadn't come along..."

"But I did." And he was thankful for that small favor from God. He gestured toward his vehicle. "Let's get you inside my car where you can feel safe."

He hustled her to the back of the Sheriff's Department vehicle and opened the door for her. She hesitated, most likely remembering the last time somebody told her to get into an SUV.

"Trust me," he murmured.

She glanced over her shoulder at him, her pretty eyes intense. "I want to." There was doubt in her voice, but she climbed inside the vehicle without further comment.

Warmth expanded within his chest. At this point he'd take whatever confidence she'd give him, even though he didn't deserve it. The sound of sirens punctuated the air. "Stay put, okay? Let us sort this out."

She settled in the seat. "I'm not going anywhere."

He left the door open so she wouldn't feel trapped and hurried to meet the sheriff, Deputy Alex Trevino, Kaitlyn and the EMT.

Taking a deep breath as the adrenaline letdown coursed through his body, Chase's legs wobbled. He tucked his thumbs into his utility belt so no one would see that his hands trembled, as well. He'd shot and killed a man.

Not something he'd ever hoped to actually do. Oh, he trained for it. They all did. Aimed for center mass as he'd been taught. Maybe if he'd shot Peters in the leg or the shoulder... He gave himself a sharp internal shake. He could've easily missed a smaller target or hit Jane. And Peters's next bullet could've torn through Chase's skull. No, he'd done the right thing.

The sheriff and Alex climbed out of the sheriff's vehicle and strode toward him. Kaitlyn joined them, having driven her own personal truck with the horse trailer behind it.

Putting his hand on Chase's shoulder, the sheriff said, "Daniel filled us in on what happened. Are you okay?"

Standing tall, Chase nodded. "Yes, sir. I will be. A little shaken."

Empathy shone in his boss's gaze. "That's to be expected. You did well."

The sheriff's praise slide inside of Chase, bolstering his confidence. "Thank you, sir."

"Alex will escort you and Miss Thompson back to the station." Sheriff Ryder turned to Kaitlyn. "You know what to do."

"Yes, sir." Kaitlyn's hazel eyes were kind as she shifted her gaze to Chase. "I'm glad you and Jane are unharmed. Please tell her I'll check in with her later."

Mild surprise washed over Chase. He hadn't known that Kaitlyn and Jane were close. "I will. How did you know to bring your horse?"

She cocked an eyebrow. "Hey, when somebody heads up the mountain with a hostage in tow, you never know when a horse might come in handy. I figured if the kidnapper took Jane deep into the forest, it would be best to be prepared to follow."

As she strode away, Chase marveled again at being blessed to be a part of the Bristle Township Sheriff's Department. Each team member was smart, competent and trustworthy. He could not have asked for better people to work with. They were like family.

"I'll drive," Alex said. He hopped into the front seat of the SUV Chase had driven up the mountain.

Not wanting to alarm Jane, Chase slid into the back seat next to her and shut the door. Jane was watching Kaitlyn ride by on her horse, a big roan with a black mane and tail. The pair stopped for a moment. Kaitlyn appeared tiny on top of the huge beast. Her blond ponytail hung down the back of her brown uniform.

"What's she doing?" Jane asked, leaning forward to watch Kaitlyn through the SUV's front window.

"Plotting out her course down the side of the mountain," Alex supplied as he started the engine.

Kaitlyn steered the large animal to the left, skirting around the metal barricade and slowly began a crisscrossed descent down the side of the hill until she disappeared from sight.

"Okay." Jane turned her troubled gaze to Chase. "But *why* is she doing that?"

"She's going to locate the body. And help coordinate the recovery from down below," Chase answered without sugarcoating the work that would need to be done.

Surprise widened her eyes. "Is that safe for her to do?"

"Kait's an accomplished horsewoman and a member of the mounted patrol," Alex replied from the front seat. "Her family breeds and trains horses. Plus, she knows this mountain like the back of her hand. She grew up here, unlike me or Chase."

"The sheriff wouldn't have asked her to do this if he weren't confident in her abilities," Chase added. "All the members of the mounted patrol are highly trained. With terrain like we have here, there are places only accessible by horseback."

"Are you on the mounted patrol?" Jane asked.

Chase met Alex's gaze in the rearview mirror. "Not yet. Alex has been teaching me how to ride. One day I hope to be trained enough to join the patrol. But for now I'm content to be ground support to the others."

"Leslie offered to give me a riding lesson," Jane said.

"You should take her up on the offer," Chase said. "She's an auxiliary member of the mounted patrol."

"Auxiliary?"

"A fancy term for volunteer," he told her. Like many western state mounted patrols, the members were a mix of paid law enforcement and trained, unarmed civilians.

"Perhaps I'll take a riding lesson." Jane turned to stare out the window. "If I live long enough to."

He didn't like to hear the despair in her tone. "You're safe, Jane."

She shook her head. "No, I'm not." She faced him. There was determination in her expression. "That man was sent to kill me. There will be more. I have to leave Bristle Township. Disappear again."

"You can't," he told her. "You said you wanted to be brave and do the right thing."

"I don't want to die," she said.

How did he get her to trust that they could protect her?

He needed to know what they were dealing with and why so they could form a plan to keep her safe. "Tell me about the night you witnessed a murder."

Dread twisted low in Ashley's gut. She blew out a breath. Dredging up the nightmare wasn't something she wanted to do but there was no way around it. Chase had to know about the monster after her. And once he learned the truth, he'd want nothing more to do with her. He'd be happy to let her slither away into the shadows.

She flicked a glance at the intimidating man named Alex in the front seat, wishing she were alone with Chase. But then again, maybe it was better that they both hear this so she wouldn't have to repeat it. "I was waitressing at an upscale restaurant in Burbank, The Matador."

Chase's eyebrows drew together. "It recently burned down, right?"

Her chest tightened. She lifted the restricting seat belt strap away from her body to suck in air. "Yes. It was reported on the news. I'm sure the fire was set because of me."

"Why would you think that?" Alex asked from the driver's seat.

She let out a small dry laugh. "Because the only person injured was the man who helped me escape California."

Chase's intense gaze locked with hers. "Did your friend know you were here in Bristle?"

Shaking her head, she said, "No. I was so careful." Remorse swamped her. "Until this morning."

"What did you do this morning?" Chase asked.

"I called the hospital where my friend was

taken." She wiped at fresh tears slipping down her cheeks. "I had to know if he was alive."

"Is he?" Chase's intense gaze locked with hers.

"For now," she said. "He's in critical condition."

Sympathy crossed Chase's face. "Were you able to talk to him?"

"No. And I didn't leave a name or number," she said. "I don't know how they found me. But they did."

"Probably tapped the hospital phone and traced the call," Alex supplied.

Her stomach knotted. She should have thought of that. Another move that put her life in jeopardy.

"Let's go to a year and a half ago," Chase urged. "What happened?"

With one hand, she pinched the bridge of her nose, forcing herself to go back to that horrible night. Her heart rate picked up as she spoke. "We were going through our closing duties like any other night. I went to take the trash out to the dumpster in the back."

She pressed her lips together for a moment as a flush of anger robbed her of speech. Finding her voice, she continued, "I forgot to put the doorstop in the door." She couldn't keep the self-recrimination from her voice. "If I had just remembered to prop the door open." She pounded her fist against her thigh. "I forgot and the door locked behind me."

His hand covered her fist. "Hey, don't be so hard on yourself. Everyone makes mistakes."

She glanced over at him and stifled a scoff. "A mistake that could get me killed."

"Not going to happen. Not on my watch."

She wanted to believe him, but there was no way he could make such a promise. Though the sentiment was heartwarming to hear and to know he meant it filled her with tenderness. But he didn't know her. And she feared if he ever really did, he'd think twice about his promises. "I'm always such a mess. I can never get anything right. I would have been fired from that job long ago if Gregor, the restaurant manager, hadn't taken a shine to me."

"A shine? Was this man taking advantage of you?"

His voice held a hard edge that startled her. His reaction gave her pause. But he was a cop. Of course his thoughts had gone to a dark place. She gave a quick shake of her head. "Oh, no. Gregor was more like a grandfather to all of us. I never knew my own grandparents. Gregor was kind and generous. He didn't deserve to be hurt."

Her words seemed to nullify the sharpness of moments before. "No, he didn't if he was willing to risk his own life to protect you." He considered her a moment. "You didn't have a spouse or boyfriend to keep you safe?"

She tucked in her chin. "Oh, none of those. I mean, I've dated, but most men either consider me more of the sister type or the best friend type."

He remained silent for a heartbeat, then said, "You took the trash out and then what happened?"

At his prompting, she refocused on telling her story. "There were people in the back alley." She bit the inside of her lip as the memory assaulted her. "Mr. Sokolov was arguing with a man."

"Who is Mr. Sokolov?"

"He owns the restaurant. I'd never seen the man he was arguing with. I tried to go back inside, but I was locked out, trapped." The helpless, vulnerable sensation she'd experienced that night was back tenfold. She smoothed her hands over her thighs, needing something to do with her hands other than wringing them like some victim.

But let's face it, she was a victim. A victim of being in the wrong place at the wrong time and seeing something that changed the course of her life.

"You must have been frightened." The fingers of his right hand laced through hers.

She held on tight, absorbing some of his strength. He was a steadfast man like a giant oak that wind could neither bend nor break. "I would have had to walk right in the middle of their argument to go around to the front of the building and be let back inside." She shuddered. "I shrank into the shadows of the garbage container, hoping they'd leave soon. But they lingered, continuing their arguing. Their voices were loud and angry."

"You heard what they were saying?"

There was no mistaking the anticipation in his tone. She hated to disappoint him.

"Some, not all. Mr. Sokolov was yelling at the man about betrayal and trusting him when he should've known better."

"This Sokolov character must have discovered the man was an undercover police officer," Chase said.

She gasped. "I didn't know. He wasn't in uniform." She tried to recall what the dead man wore. "He had on jeans, a T-shirt and baseball cap."

"His clothing would make sense if he was undercover," Chase said.

"Where was his backup?" Alex asked.

"That's a good question," Chase answered. "One we'll have to ask Chief Macintosh." Chase returned his attention to her. "Go on."

"Mr. Sokolov reached underneath his coat and pulled out a gun." The memory made her shrink a bit, her shoulders rounding and her chin dipping. She wanted to forget, to curl in a ball and pretend she hadn't seen any of it.

"You saw this?" Alex asked.

"Yes." She lifted her face and met Chase's gaze. "He shot that man. I had to bite my fist to keep from screaming."

Chase squeezed her hands.

Tears rolled down her cheeks. Anxiety fluttered in her chest. "The sight of that man crumbling to the ground and Mr. Sokolov stepping over the man he'd just killed like he was a piece of garbage will be forever etched in my brain."

Now she could add watching the phony detective going over the side of the cliff. Definitely, the stuff of nightmares.

"So you ran away?"

"Not at first. After Mr. Sokolov was gone, I ran to the man to offer help. But he had no pulse. And there was so much blood." She remembered gagging at the sight. "Then I heard a noise and ran back behind the garbage bin. Gregor found me there. He hustled me away from the restaurant."

"Did someone remove the body?" Alex asked.

She glanced toward Alex and met his gaze in the rearview mirror. "I don't know. I didn't hear anyone else and I didn't want to look again."

Chase's eyebrows dipped together. "How does Sokolov know you witnessed the crime?"

She'd wondered that, too. Had Gregor revealed her secret to Sokolov? No, wait. "Didn't you say Peters, or whoever he was, had a photo of me leaving the back door of The Matador?"

"He did," Chase answered. "But if you worked there, why wouldn't they have known your name?"

She shrugged, sadness filling her chest. "I can only guess Gregor took me out of the system and that the others…" She swallowed back the choking sensation in her throat. "They must have covered for me."

And risked their lives. For her. Why would

anyone do that if that wasn't their job? She couldn't fathom it. But she couldn't deny the warmth layering upon her fear. The people she'd worked with had protected her. There was no way for her to ever repay them.

"How long before the police arrived?" Alex asked.

She bit her lip. "I didn't see any police."

"Surely someone would have reported hearing a gunshot," Chase stated.

She cocked her head, trying to recall more of that night. "It's strange. I don't remember hearing the gun go off."

"The weapon could have had a noise suppressor like the guy today," Chase told her. "But even those make a sound that would have likely echoed through the alley."

She didn't know what to say to that. She'd been frightened, her heart pounding so loud in her ears and her breathing labored from terror.

"What did you hear?" Chase pressed.

"I—I don't recall." She searched her mind, desperate to dredge up some answer, but there was nothing, just the looping images and the residual fear. "It was a year and a half ago. But I know what I saw."

"Are you sure it was Sokolov who fired the fatal shot?" Alex asked, as he parked the vehicle in front of the sheriff's station, a brick two-story structure that had been rebuilt after a fire last year.

Ashley couldn't see any signs of the damage done by the blaze. The image of The Matador flittered through her thoughts and grief over what was lost twisted in her chest. "Yes." There was no doubt in her mind about Mr. Sokolov's guilt.

Alex twisted in his seat to study her. "Did the other guy have a weapon?"

She shook her head, embarrassed for not knowing the answer. "Not that I noticed."

"Why didn't you go to the police?" Chase asked. "That would have been the best course of action."

Stung by his words and the fact that she hadn't done the *best course of action*, she tried to explain. "I wanted to. Once the shock of it all wore off, my first instinct was to run to the nearest police station." Her lips twisted. "But Gregor… He said I couldn't trust the police. Mr. Sokolov owned too many of them. Gregor said I couldn't trust anyone."

"But you trusted Gregor," Chase pointed out.

Ashley detected a hint of complaint in his

voice. "I did. He was my friend and had helped me. But he couldn't protect me long-term. Mr. Sokolov was cruel. Gregor had a scar on his face given to him by Mr. Sokolov when he'd let one of the waiters leave early because his child was sick. Everyone was afraid of Mr. Sokolov."

"Why did any of you stay there?" Alex asked, his gaze genuinely puzzled.

She shrugged. "He paid well." She focused back at Chase, taking comfort in his attention. "And when Mr. Sokolov wasn't around, it was a great place to work."

Chase's gaze intensified. "Then why run?"

Her chin dropped a fraction. "Gregor said my only option to stay alive was to run, keep moving and never look back. Mr. Sokolov would kill me and everyone I loved."

A scowl dipped Chase's eyebrows together as if he didn't like what she'd said. Neither did she. Being on the run, looking over her shoulder, constantly afraid had wreaked havoc with her mind.

"How did you survive this last year and a half?" Chase asked.

"Gregor gave me some cash, and the identification of a woman my approximate age and

height and put me on a bus for New Mexico."
Those first few days were beyond stressful.

His gaze narrowed. He slid his hands from
hers. "Wait, are you telling me you're not Jane
Thompson?"

The moment she'd dreaded had arrived. It
was said that the truth will set you free, but she
had a sickening quiver in the pit of her stomach that, in this case, the truth would condemn
her. Would he still want to help her, knowing
she'd deceived him and everyone else?

THREE

Chase's breath stalled in his lungs. He sat back to stare at the woman sitting beside him, taking in the paleness of her complexion, her short curly hair and frightened eyes. She wasn't who she'd said she was. "What is your real name?"

Her lips twisted in a rueful grimace. She ducked her chin slightly. "Ashley Willis."

He rubbed the back of his neck as he absorbed this bit of information. She'd lied about her identity. Was she still lying? How did he even know if she was telling him her real name? Or if the story she'd just told him and Alex was true? Was she mixed up in something that had ended the life of a police officer? Or had she really witnessed his death, as she claimed? Chase didn't like all the questions and doubts. He wanted to believe she was now telling the truth. Should he give her the benefit of the doubt?

"Ashley." He said the name slowly, testing it. "It will take some getting used to."

"At first it was hard to remember to answer to Jane."

Exchanging a glance with Alex, Chase replied, "I would imagine. Living a lie would be difficult."

"It was necessary to stay alive." She met his gaze with a direct look. "I couldn't even go back to the apartment I shared with three other women." Sadness crept across her pretty, tear-stained face. "I can't imagine what they are thinking. Gregor assured me he'd take care of my things, so I hope he told them I'd landed an acting gig and was moving up in the world."

His stomach dropped. It was an actress's job to lie, in a way. No wonder she'd pulled off being Jane so long. "You're an actress?"

"Aspiring. I did a few commercials." Her mouth twisted. "Mostly I'm a waitress. Just like my mother."

"Where is she?" Alex asked.

She glanced at him. "Barstow, California."

Alex tilted his head. "Does she know where you are?"

Jane—uh, Ashley, shook her head. "I didn't want to put her in danger." She shrugged as a flash of hurt lit her eyes. "I doubt she'd care to know where I was, anyway."

Chase couldn't decide if she was courageous or foolish. Or playing him. "How did you end up here in Bristle Township?"

"I first landed in Albuquerque, then went on to Santa Fe. Every few weeks I kept moving. I intended to head to Canada. But by the time I arrived here, I was nearly out of cash. And I didn't know what else to do, so I rented a room and got a job."

"You did the smart thing by staying put." If the assassin had found her somewhere else, things might not have ended well for her. "Now, you have to do another smart and brave thing. You need to go back to Burbank and testify about what you saw."

She shook her head, terror darkening her eyes. "He'll kill me just like he did that man. You've already seen he's determined. Please, the best thing for me is to keep moving."

He couldn't let her disappear. There were too many unanswered questions. "I understand your fear. You were alone and on the run. But no longer. You have me and the Sheriff's Department watching your back."

His words didn't seem to reassure her. He

dared to press, "You need to tell the authorities in Los Angeles what you told us."

A visible shudder rippled through her. "But what if the police there can't protect me?"

Knowing he was taking a chance that might backfire, he said, "I'll be there with you."

Her eyebrows rose. "You mean, you'd actually go with me to LA? Won't that interfere with your job here?"

"You let me worry about my job." He ignored Alex's snort from the front seat.

Chase had no doubt the sheriff would allow him to take his vacation days to accompany Ashley to Los Angeles. Whatever it took for her to feel secure in doing the right thing. His heart ached for her, for the hardship she'd endured and the horror she had witnessed. One thing he knew was that the trauma she'd gone through today was real. Someone wanted her dead. And guilt for letting the danger get so close to her ate at him. But it was time for her to come clean and help law enforcement put away a criminal. Getting her to agree to testify might take some work. Regardless, he would persevere.

She shook her head. "I can't ask that of you. I've deceived you. I don't deserve your sympathy or your protection." She lifted her chin high as if she were ready to take a punch to the jaw.

His stomach contracted. Had someone hit this woman in the past? Or was this all bravado? Did she think she deserved to take her lumps for hiding her identity? Did she really expect them to turn their backs on her? Empathy nipped at him. She had to be telling the truth. No one could fake that kind of fear. And the danger was real.

He gathered her hands once again in his. "You were doing what you had to to survive. No one can fault you for that."

She relaxed, blinking rapidly. "I should have gone to the police and taken my chances."

He agreed, but what was done was done. They had to move forward. "You were in shock. You witnessed something horrible. When people are in the middle of trauma, they don't make the best choices. And you were given advice that may, or may not, have saved your life."

She turned away from him. "That's true. Once I ran, I knew there was no going back."

"But there is," Chase insisted. "Once you testify to what you saw."

Alex popped open the driver's side door. "We should get her inside."

Chase helped Ashley from the vehicle and ushered her into the sheriff's station. "You'll stay here for the time being. Safer that way."

She nodded. "Good. I don't want to put Mrs. Marsh in danger. But I should tell my boss at the Java Bean."

"We'll call him later and explain." He directed her to the chair next to his desk. "From now on, I'm sticking to you like glue. We're in this together."

He was rewarded with tears and a wobbly smile. "Thank you," she whispered. "I've been alone so long."

"Not anymore." He grabbed the phone. "Right now, I'm going to call Chief Macintosh and find out exactly what is going on."

She put her hand on his arm. "Can you call the hospital and check on Gregor?" Her gaze beseeched him to comply. "He helped me when he didn't have to and he asked for nothing in return. It would make me feel better if I knew he was doing okay. That they haven't harmed him trying to get to me."

For some reason her devotion to this man irritated Chase. He marshaled the strange reaction. It was a small thing to do, considering all she'd been through. A favor he was willing to grant. His heart squeezed tight. "Of course."

She gave him the name of the hospital. A quick internet search gave him the hospital's main number. He identified himself and inquired about Gregor Kominski's condition.

What he heard sent his stomach plummeting. He thanked the woman and hung up. Turning to Ashley, he said, "I'm sorry to tell you this. Gregor Kominski succumbed to his injuries."

Gregor was dead.

Anguish tore through Ashley. She dropped her head into her hands as grief swelled, making her insides ache. Gregor had died because of her. Guilt like shards of glass embedded themselves into her heart. He died even though he hadn't known where she was and yet Mr. Sokolov found her through him, anyway.

Gregor's death had accomplished what Mr. Sokolov had intended. He'd found her. And he'd sent someone to kill her. A shudder of terror worked over her limbs. How many more killers would show up until she was dead?

Gentle hands landed on her shoulders. "Ashley, you are not responsible for what happened to your friend."

She lifted her gaze to meet Chase's. How did he know that she blamed herself? Was she that easy to read? Or was he that good at his job? She suspected it was the latter.

This man was so kind, so generous and honorable. She didn't deserve his help. And if anything happened to him… Her heart contracted painfully in her chest.

If anything happened to anyone in Bristle Township because of her, she would not be able to live with herself. Especially now that she had let down her guard enough to allow people in, even if only just a little. She'd made ties to this community that she'd never intended to form. That had to end here and now.

She gave Chase a tight smile. "I appreciate your trying to comfort me. But I know Mr. Sokolov is the guilty party. And he needs to pay."

For the first time since that night, the seeds of anger took root, making her limbs shake. She wanted desperately to be brave enough to bring Mr. Sokolov down.

She needed a moment to collect herself. "Is there a restroom I can use?"

"Down the corridor, door on your left," Chase instructed.

On wobbly legs, she made her way down the hall as the sheriff returned. Quickly, she ducked into the restroom, not ready to have a face-to-face with Chase's boss.

Once inside the small single-user space, she turned the lock and slumped against the door as the floodgates let loose and she sobbed into her hands. She was crying for herself and for her friend who had paid the ultimate price. It was all so unfair. But then she knew God never promised fair.

She wasn't naive. Even if Mr. Sokolov were behind bars, her life would be in danger.

Fair or not, she would have to leave Bristle Township. A deep cold numbness spread through her body.

She couldn't allow anyone here to get any more involved with her. She couldn't allow her heart to become more attached than it already was. There would come a point when she would find an opportunity to leave.

Until then, she would do what was necessary to keep everyone safe. And she would pray, with everything in her, that the handsome deputy would be able to protect her long enough to give her testimony. Then she would disappear again, despite how much her heart longed to stay in Bristle Township.

She left the restroom and headed back to Chase's desk, only he wasn't there. A flutter of anxiety hit her in the gut. Then she spied him in the sheriff's office talking with his boss. She put a hand to her stomach to quell the uneasy knot camping out there.

"Is it true?" Deputy Kaitlyn Lanz walked in. Her blond hair was mussed with little twigs sticking out from the long strands. Her uniform also showed signs of her trek into the forest and the distinct smell of horseflesh wafted in the air, teasing Ashley's nose. She sneezed.

"Alex told me your story," Kaitlyn said.

Ashley's heart thudded in her chest. Kaitlyn stared at her, waiting for an answer.

Swallowing back the bile rising to burn her throat, Ashley had no illusions that once she confirmed the truth, Kaitlyn wouldn't want to have anything more to do with her. She braced herself. "Yes, it's true. I'm not Jane Thompson. My name is Ashley Willis." The burn of tears pricked her eyes. "I'm so, so sorry."

Kaitlyn came to her and wrapped her in a hug.

Surprise rendered Ashley immobile, even as her nose twitched again with the urge to sneeze.

Drawing back to meet Ashley's gaze, Kaitlyn stated in her no-nonsense tone, "I would have done the same."

Kaitlyn's kindness made Ashley want to cry. "I hated not telling you."

"Don't apologize for doing what you had to. I'm just glad that we know and now we can help you." One corner of Kaitlyn's mouth tipped upward. "Ashley, huh?"

Ashley nodded.

"Okay, then," Kaitlyn said. "You're a survivor. A fighter. I can respect that."

As much as Ashley wanted to believe Kaitlyn's words, she knew they weren't true. If she'd had any backbone, she'd have gone to the authorities in the beginning and not lost a year and a half of her life to fear.

Chase stepped out of the sheriff's private office and joined them.

Putting her arm around Ashley, Kaitlyn addressed Chase, "So what are we going to do to protect our friend?"

A small smile played at the corners of his mouth. "Bless you, Kait."

Kaitlyn's eyebrows rose. "What? You thought I'd turn my back on someone in trouble?"

Chase shook his head. "Actually, no." His gaze met Ashley's. "But I have a suspicion someone else might have had that thought."

Heat rose in Ashley's cheeks. She had expected the worst. Better to be pessimistic than to hope for the best and be disappointed.

Kaitlyn bumped her with her shoulder. "We good?"

Bemused, Ashley bumped her back. "Yes." For now. However, she really had to find a way to put some distance between them all so none of them were hurt. But for the life of her, she couldn't bring herself to pull away.

"She can stay with me," Kaitlyn announced.

"Actually, the Los Angeles district attorney, Evan Nyburg, is making arrangements for us to fly to California in the morning," Chase told them.

"You're going with her?" Kaitlyn asked.

Ashley held her breath. He'd promised to not abandon her, but she wasn't sure that was a promise he could keep.

"Yes," Chase confirmed.

"The sheriff is okay with that?" Ashley blurted out the question.

"Yes, he's on board for me to escort you to Los Angeles. The district attorney's office is arranging hotel rooms at the Denver airport for tonight and tickets on the first plane out in the morning."

"Good," Kaitlyn said.

"Kaitlyn," the sheriff called from the doorway of his office and waved her over.

"Excuse me, the boss calls." Kaitlyn left them to join the sheriff in his office.

Ashley put her hand on Chase's arm. "I don't know what to say. You shouldn't be taking time away from your work for me."

"Ashley, I'm doing my job. Keeping you safe is a priority." The phone on his desk rang. "I'm expecting a call."

While Chase took his call, Ashley marveled at the way these people were rallying around her. It didn't make any sense to her. In her limited experience, very few people would go out of their way to assist a stranger.

But they had signed up to do just that, she reasoned. And she shouldn't read anything more into their willingness to help her. She needed to keep an emotional barrier up and the best way for her to do that was to remember Chase and Kaitlyn were being paid to protect and serve.

Chase hung up the phone, his expression troubled. Dread filled Ashley. What now?

Chase stared at his desk phone for a moment, pondering the upsetting news he'd just learned. Ashley sat in the chair beside his desk, drawing his attention. He was glad to see she'd pulled herself together. He'd sensed she was on the verge of a breakdown when she'd hurried to the restroom. Empathy curled through Chase. Her guilt had been palpable when he'd told her of Gregor's demise. Chase hoped she really understood that the blame for her friend's death laid at the feet of the one who set the fire and the one who'd ordered the deed done.

"Is everything okay?" she asked.

He ran a hand over his stubbled jaw. "That was Detective Peters's boss. The real Detective Peters," he amended, because they didn't have a name yet for the man Chase shot. "Macintosh is sending over some photos and I want you to see if you can identify the man you saw killed."

Her chin dipped. "Do you think it might not have been Detective Peters?"

"Honestly, I don't know what to think. Did you know that Sokolov is believed to be the head of a drug cartel with ties to Eastern Europe?"

"No." Surprise colored her voice. "I never saw any drugs at the restaurant."

The ding of an incoming email drew his gaze to his computer screen. He opened the post from Chief Macintosh and clicked on the attachment. An image appeared with two rows of four mug shots, each one numbered. Chase didn't know which was the real detective.

He turned the monitor so Ashley could see the pictures. "Take your time," he told her.

She stared at the screen with uncertainty written across her face. "He was far away and it was dark."

"But not too dark for you to see Sokolov?"

"There was a street lamp. Mr. Sokolov was standing beneath it, but the other man was shadowed."

"Close your eyes and go back to that night if it helps."

She did as he suggested and after a moment she opened her eyes. Taking control of the mouse, she blew up each photo and stared at it, before moving on to the next one. Finally on photo number seven, she sat back. "That was him. I'm sure of it."

"I'll let Macintosh know," he said. He sent off a quick email, telling the chief the witness had identified photo number seven.

A few seconds later, Macintosh replied. Chase read the email. "You've identified Detective Peters. The detective went rogue. They don't know why he was there in the alley that night. He told no one of his plans. Thus why there was no backup."

She winced. "Do you think he was dirty?"

Chase hoped not. "Hard to say at this point. It would really help if you could remember anything that the detective said."

"I've been trying," she said. "His voice was more of a murmur so I don't recall his exact words. But Mr. Sokolov didn't appear to be concerned with anybody hearing him."

Chase read the rest of the email. "Detective Peters's body was found dumped in the ocean and washed up on shore. If that hadn't happened, he would still be missing."

There was no mistaking the surprise in Ashley's red-rimmed eyes. "Someone moved him. And..." She grimaced.

She didn't need to state the rest. Yes, someone had tried to cover up the crime. "Are you sure, without a doubt, it was Maksim Sokolov who pulled the trigger?" Even though Alex had asked the question earlier, Chase needed to reaffirm her answer.

"Yes, I'm sure."

Chase was glad to hear her confidence.

She heaved a sigh. "Okay. Now you all know who was shot, when and where. Do I have to go back to LA?"

"Yes, you do. The district attorney wants to depose you himself and then at some point you'll have to appear before a grand jury, then in court."

She made a pained face. "He'll be there, in court, right?"

Chase wasn't going to sugarcoat the truth. "If we can make the charges stick and take him to trial. Then yes, Sokolov will be in the courtroom and he will be watching you. But you don't have to speak to him. All you'll need to do is testify that he was the one you saw pull the trigger."

"You'll be with me?"

He understood her concern. The case could take months if not years to go to trial. "I promise. No matter how long it takes."

"But what about your job?" The distress in her tone was touching.

"You let me worry about that. I'll work it out with the sheriff." Not wanting to examine why he'd make such a promise, he turned off his computer and gathered his personal belongings. "Come on. We'll head to my place. I need to pack a bag and change into clean clothes before we head to Denver."

"My duffel bag?"

"It's still in the SUV. We'll grab it on the

way to my truck." He paused. "I'll need to text Lucinda to let her know we're on our way."

Ashley's eyebrows rose. "Who's Lucinda? Your wife?"

"No, the woman who raised me," he said. After sending the text, he put his hand to the small of Ashley's back and led her outside. "Lucinda Jones was my nanny as a child. When I moved here, I brought her with me. Her husband passed several years ago, and she didn't want to move to Florida where her adult son and his family reside."

"What about your parents?"

"They live in Chicago. Dad's a cardiologist and Mom's the hospital administrator." And not really a part of his life except for on holidays. They were too consumed by their professions.

After retrieving her bag, he helped her climb into his truck, a blue metallic 1987 Silverado pickup.

Once they were on the road, she smoothed a hand over the dashboard. "This is pretty cool."

He smiled. "Thanks."

"I think one of my mom's boyfriends had one of these back in the day."

He slanted her a quick glance. "Were there many boyfriends?"

Ashley sat back and gripped the edge of the bucket seat. "Yes. My mother is a difficult and complicated woman."

He understood difficult and complicated. Two words he could attribute to his own parents. "What about your father?"

"I was a baby when he left." She turned her head away. "Did you restore the truck yourself?"

Clearly, she didn't want to talk about her family. There would be time to assuage his curiosity about Ashley. But for now the truck was a neutral topic.

"I did." He couldn't keep the pride out of his tone. "Rebuilding the truck was a labor of love and a challenge. It was one of my first purchases when I arrived in Bristle Township. I needed something to get me around, but I didn't want anything fancy. And because I was low on funds, I bought this beast from a local farmer who had it sitting in a barn. Over the next year or so, I refurbished her every night and weekend."

Ashley's laugh filled the cab as her gaze swung to him. "You call the truck a *her*?"

Enjoying the sound of her laugh, he said, "Yep. Blue Belle."

"Hello, Blue Belle."

Her smile tugged at him. Not for the first time, he battled the draw of attraction. She was so pretty. He recalled her words about men not thinking of her in terms of dating, only as the friend or the sister. He hated to think she didn't believe herself to be beautiful and attractive. But it wasn't his place to inform her that she was both. His job was to protect her.

He pulled into the driveway of his one-level mid-century modern home with a small yard and shut off the engine.

"Nice place," she commented.

"Thank you. It was a fixer-upper when I bought it. Someday I plan to get a dog but just haven't taken the time." He climbed out and came around to her side of the cab to open her door. She didn't move. "Ashley?"

"What if he sends more assassins after me? I shouldn't be here. I shouldn't be putting you and Lucinda in danger."

"I can't leave you out here," he said. "We won't be long." He held out his hand. "Lucinda will have dinner ready. And we don't want to keep her waiting."

As they entered the house, Chase couldn't stop from glancing over his shoulder at the quiet residential street as Ashley's words rang through his head. There was validity to her fear.

What were the chances that a man like Sokolov would only send one assassin to Bristle Township?

FOUR

Ashley savored each bite of the home-cooked meal of spaghetti and meatballs as if it were her last. Which, she thought somewhat morbidly, it could be if more hit men came after her. All the more reason to eat every last bite.

After arriving at Chase's house and being introduced to the woman whom he shared the place with, Ashley had freshened up, putting on a clean light-weight pink sweater and cotton slacks, then helped get the meal on the table. "Thank you so much for this deliciousness," she said to the elderly woman sitting in a wheelchair at the end of the table.

"I'm so glad you enjoyed it." Lucinda Jones's dark eyes twinkled with pleasure. "Can't send you and Chase off on an empty stomach."

Ashley put her hand to her full tummy. "No chance of that."

"We won't be gone for too long," Chase assured the woman. He'd showered, shaved and changed out of his uniform into jeans that fit his lean form well. His sandy blond hair, still damp at the ends, curled at his nape. The plaid shirt in hues of blue deepened the color of his blue eyes. "A day or two at the most."

Ashley wasn't sure he should be making such a promise on her behalf. Once she arrived back in Los Angeles, she might not be returning to Colorado. The district attorney may want her to stay put. Or at the very least, she would be heading off to another new place where she could disappear, until it was time to testify in open court.

She suppressed a shiver of dread. There was still much to do before that horrible day arrived. First, they needed to drive to Denver and fly to southern California where she would be deposed by the district attorney. So many things could go wrong between here and there. And Chase knew it, too. She'd seen the way he'd secured the house, making sure every window was shut, every door locked and the curtains pulled closed.

Chase's cell phone trilled from inside his front shirt pocket.

Lucinda arched an eyebrow.

He shrugged. "I'm expecting this. I have to

take it." He rose from the table. "Excuse me." He walked away, his deep voice low as he answered the call.

Lucinda used the toggle on the console of her electric wheelchair to move closer to Ashley. She touched Ashley's arm. "Chase tells me you're in some trouble."

Startled, Ashley stared at the woman. "Yes. How much did he tell you?"

"No details, just enough for me to know to pray for you both."

For some reason the older woman's words caused Ashley's throat to close. She quickly drank from her water goblet, letting the cool liquid calm her throat and push back the rising tide of emotion. She couldn't remember ever having anyone pray specifically for her. When she was sure she had control over her vocals, she said, "I appreciate your prayers. I'm not sure I deserve them."

"Everyone deserves to be held in prayer," Lucinda responded with a pat on Ashley's arm.

Not wanting to debate the point, Ashley decided to give in to her curiosity and said, "You were Chase's nanny."

A smile crinkled the corners of Lucinda's eyes. "Yes. I started taking care of him not long after he was born. He was the crankiest, loudest baby ever."

Adjectives that Ashley wouldn't have attributed to the man she was getting to know. "But you have your own children?"

"I do. A son. He was ten when I went to work for the Fredrick family. After my husband passed, I no longer had a reason to stay in Chicago, but didn't want to go south to Florida where my son and his family now live. Too hot. I prefer to have seasons. Chase was a dear to invite me to come here."

A dear. What an apt phrase. "How long did you care for Chase?"

"Until high school," Lucinda answered. "Even then, he would show up on our doorstep more often than not."

"It beat eating alone," Chase interjected as he returned. "That was one of the district attorney's assistants. Everything's all arranged. She's texting me the flight information and the hotel confirmation."

No sooner had he said the words than a ding from his phone let them know the text had arrived.

Ashley was more interested in learning about Chase. "Your parents weren't home for dinner?" Not that her own mother had been home or made dinner often, but she'd imagined that Chase grew up with two attentive parents when they weren't working.

"Rarely." He picked up their empty plates and strode into the kitchen.

"If Chase were a different kind of man, he could've gotten himself into some serious trouble," Lucinda said as she backed her chair away from the table.

Chase stepped into the arched doorway between the dining room and kitchen, wiping his hands on a towel. "You taught me well, Lucinda. Hard work and service for others is what life is about. Not partying like most of my peers."

Lucinda beamed. "Yes and look at you now. You're a fine deputy." She turned to Ashley, pinning her with an intent stare. "A fine catch."

Ashley smothered a choked laugh. She had no words to respond with.

"Enough, Lucinda." Chase tossed the towel onto the counter and walked fully into the dining room. Amusement sparked in his eyes. "She's hoping I will find someone to settle down with. But I am settled. My life's just about perfect the way it is."

Something strange twisted in Ashley's gut.

Lucinda snorted. "You keep telling yourself that. I'd like some babies to cuddle." She winked at Ashley. "I like to tease him. But I can't wait for him to have more in his life than work."

"I'm sure he will." Except she wouldn't be here to see it.

Settle down. Babies. All normal, healthy things for anyone to want. A longing from some place deep inside of Ashley tugged for attention, but she staunchly ignored the pull. Her life would never be normal. Not that she even knew what that was. Her childhood had been chaotic and at times scary.

Besides, a family of her own wasn't something she could dream about, not when there was a man out there bent on killing her.

She would never be safe enough to have a life free from fear. The thought made her shoulders droop and fatigue set in.

Shaking his head with good-natured humor at Lucinda's not so subtle matchmaking, Chase kissed the older woman's cheek. "It's time that we head out." He straightened and held out his hand to Ashley. "We'll make it to the airport hotel just after dark."

Slipping her hand into his, Ashley cherished the comforting and warm contact as he helped her to her feet. The world spun and for a moment she clung to him.

His concerned gaze made her withdraw her hand and plant her feet as her equilibrium returned. "Head rush. Happens sometimes."

Accepting her explanation with a nod, he moved to grab their bags from the couch and walked outside.

Ashley bent to hug Lucinda. "Again, thank you. It was lovely to meet you."

"And you, dear," the older woman said. "I'll lift you both up in prayer. And you can be assured Chase will keep you safe."

But at what cost? Ashley stifled the question, not wanting to cause Lucinda any undue worry. Closing the door behind her, Ashley hurried to the truck. Chase stowed their bags behind the bucket seats. From a holster hidden beneath the right pant leg of his jeans, he removed a gun.

She noticed it wasn't the same sort of weapon he'd been carrying earlier. This one was smaller but she was sure just as lethal. He put the gun in the glove box.

"It's my personal weapon. I had to surrender my service sidearm at the station."

Her stomach clenched. He'd shot someone

to protect her today. She hoped and prayed he wouldn't have to do that again.

"Are you close with your parents now that you're an adult?" she asked, hoping to learn more about this man she was trusting her life with.

He started up the engine and backed out of the driveway. Once on the road, he answered, "Not especially. Don't get me wrong. I love them. They're great people. They've accomplished so much. I just don't know them, and they don't really know me. Kind of hard to build a relationship when they were gone so much of the time."

"That must've been hard for you. But you had Lucinda." What she wouldn't have given to have someone like Lucinda in her life.

He darted a glance her way. "It was hard, I suppose. I didn't know any different. But you're right, I had Lucinda and her family. They became my family. And I much preferred their brownstone to the big house on the lake."

She couldn't imagine living a life with so many choices. "I grew up in a trailer park," she blurted out.

"No shame in that."

She smiled to herself. Old wounds ached but

she'd learned to hold her head high in spite of the circumstances of her past. "*You* can say that because you didn't live it. In school I was considered trailer trash. What was even more ironic was that our trailer actually sat next to the trash bins. Even the other kids in the trailer park called me trailer trash."

His jaw hardened. "Children can be mean."

"True."

"I was called less than complimentary names at my school."

"You were?" She would have thought he'd have been part of the popular kids. "I can't believe that."

His shoulders rose and fell. "Except for one stint on the football team my freshman year of high school, I kept to myself. I didn't want anyone to know who my parents were."

"Why not? They are successful and rich from the sound of it." She'd have told everyone and been giddy to have the life he'd led.

"Exactly. Once people knew, then they treated me differently. Or wanted something from me."

Her heart hurt to think that Chase had had so much yet had been unhappy. "Money doesn't buy happiness."

"Not for me. I would rather have had my parents' attention than a big house and fancy clothes."

"I can understand that."

"You had your mom. Was she a good mother?"

Ashley turned the question over in her mind. She had nothing to compare her childhood to other than what she'd seen on television or read in books. "I want to believe she tried but nurturing wasn't natural for her. Not like with your Lucinda."

Even in the short time Ashley had spent with Chase's former nanny, she'd been cared for and treated like she was special.

"My mother wasn't the most nurturing, either," Chase said. "She ran a large organization with a lot of balls in the air. She didn't know what to do with a child under foot."

"I doubt your mom was free with her fists or her criticism." As soon as the words were out, she wanted to retract them. She didn't want him to pity her.

"She hurt you?"

His quiet tone filled with indignation on her behalf was more compelling than knowing he was doing his job to protect her. She wanted to laugh off the volatile nature of her mother but she couldn't find it within herself to be less than honest with Chase. "Sometimes. She was a single parent raising a child she'd never wanted."

He made a noise she took as sympathy.

"Don't get me wrong, we would do some mother-daughter things, like give ourselves pedicures or have movie nights with popcorn and candy." The memories were faded and frayed at the edges, but not forgotten. Those were the times Ashley had treasured. "There were many nights when she didn't come home." A shiver raced over her skin. She'd hated being alone in the trailer.

Chase's hands gripped and re-gripped the steering wheel. "Wasn't there anyone to help you? A grandparent or neighbor?"

She smoothed her hands over her thighs. "Not really. As soon as I was old enough, I would bike to the library as much as possible. I found solace in the books. And had many wonderful adventures sitting in the alcove of the Barstow library."

"I'm glad you had someplace to retreat to when it was scary at home. Though it pains me to think of you mistreated by the one person who should have been sheltering you from the ugliness of the world."

She stared at him, mesmerized by his profile. He was handsome in so many ways. His kindheartedness was so sweet and appealing. She was thankful God had put Chase in her path.

After a long beat of silence, Chase said, "I spent a great deal of time at the library, too, when I wasn't with Lucinda's family."

Grateful to have the subject change from her childhood to his, she commented, "I noticed your bookshelves. Many classics, as well as popular fiction."

"A book doesn't judge or betray you," he stated.

"Or hurt you." She wondered if he was only referring to his childhood. Had he loved someone who then betrayed him? "Why haven't you settled down?"

He groaned. "Not you, too."

"I'm just curious. And surprised. You're a catch." The words slipped out and flooded her with embarrassment. "I mean, not for me. I'm not looking to catch you." She was digging herself a deeper hole.

His soft laugh filled the cab of the truck. "I'm not sure if I should be insulted or not."

"No! I didn't mean to be insulting." Remorse for her words made her pulse pound.

He slanted her a glance. "I'm teasing. In all seriousness, dating was painful as a teen. I was never sure if the girls were interested in me as a person or in my last name. And in college I was too focused on graduating quickly so I could join the Chicago Police Department. I never took the time for a relationship. And wasn't sure I could trust someone to love me for me. What about you?"

She related to not knowing if she could trust someone to love her unconditionally. "My focus was getting out of Barstow. As soon as I turned eighteen, I escaped to Los Angeles."

"Did you always want to be an actress?"

"What little girl doesn't when they're young?" She could remember wanting to be a part of a television family so badly she'd ached. "One of the girls in the house I ended up living in introduced me to her agent. For the next few years, I went on auditions. I landed a few bit parts here and there. Hard to learn the craft with no money for acting lessons. I wasn't a natural. The camera was intimidating, plus having all the people on set watching you, judging you." She made a face. "Only significant thing I did was a commercial for a national car company."

"I'll have to search for it on the internet. How did you end up at The Matador?"

"To pay the bills I started waiting tables. First at a fast food joint and then a pizza parlor. One of my housemates worked at The Matador and when a position opened up, she told me about it." For a time she'd thought she'd won the best prize ever. Then that horrible night happened, and her world spun out of control.

"Did you not want to go to college?"

She had, so badly. "Kind of hard to do without money."

"You could have applied for scholarships or financial aid."

She sighed. "I didn't know how to apply for them." And had no one to ask.

"It's not too late, you know. Nowadays you can take classes online and receive a degree."

There was no point in dreaming when her life would be about staying hidden from Maksim Sokolov. "What did you study in college?"

"Communications. It was a compromise with my parents. There was no way I wanted to be a doctor or administrator. I wanted to be a police officer. Lucinda's father was a retired Chicago detective. He would tell us stories of his time on the force. And I knew that that's what I wanted to do. I wanted to serve others, just not the way my parents did."

She appreciated Chase's honor and integrity. And his desire to do for others without any real compensation beyond his pay. He wasn't posturing for accolades. She liked that about him. Back in Los Angeles, the guys she'd met all wanted to be the center of attention. "At one time I thought I might want to be a librarian."

A smile spread across his face. "You could, you know. Mrs. Hawkins is always asking for volunteers at the library."

Turning her gaze to the window, she said, "Maybe someday." Only not in Bristle Township. The thought hurt.

The truck sped up, pushing her back against the seat. She glanced at Chase. He sat straighter; tension radiated off him and made the fine hairs on her arms jump with alarm. "What's wrong?"

"I think we are being followed," he said. "There's a sedan that has been keeping the same distance behind us since we left town. Every time I slow down, they slow down. When I speed up, so do they."

She twisted in her seat to stare out the rear window at the dark car. "What should we do?"

Before he could answer, the sedan raced forward and kissed the bumper of the truck. The hit jerked Ashley forward. She let out a yelp of panic. Chase floored it, and the truck strained for more speed.

"Grab my phone from my front shirt pocket."

She reached for it, but the seat belt slammed her back against the seat. Quickly, she shrugged out from beneath the chest strap and managed to pluck the cell phone from his shirt pocket. "There's only one bar." Cell coverage in the mountains was spotty at best.

"We have to pray we can get through. Press one and enter."

Please let the call connect. She did as instructed. She could hear it ringing.

"Put it on speaker," he said.

She pressed the speaker button just as a woman's voice filled the cab, "Bristle County Sheriff's Department, Carole speaking."

"Chase here. Listen, we need help. Mile marker 15 headed. A dark sedan is trying to force us to crash."

"I'll tell the sheriff—"

The line went dead. Panic seized Ashley. Her breathing turned shallow. "They won't arrive in time."

"Brace yourself," Chase instructed tightly.

"I have to get us off the road before they cause an accident."

Ashley grabbed the door handle with one hand and the dashboard with the other. At the last possible moment, Chase cranked the wheel, crossing the oncoming traffic lane and taking a graveled road on squealing tires. They shot down the road through the trees, gravel flying in their wake.

Ashley kept an eye on the side-view mirror. For what seemed like a long moment, she held her breath, praying the car would pass by and keep going.

The sedan made the turn. The truck bounced, and she barely hung onto the phone. Ashley's breath hitched. "Now what?"

Chase pressed hard on the gas. The truck shot forward. The road began to climb. Behind them the car sped up.

"They're gaining on us!" Ashley's hands curled into fists. It wasn't fair. She should never have allowed Chase to talk her into this. If he had let her leave on the bus this morning, he wouldn't be in danger now.

"Hang on!" He yanked on the wheel, taking a hard right and going off road into the trees.

She clutched the phone, panic making her breathing shallow and her head spin.

"Ashley!" Chase's voice whipped through the cab, coercing her to focus. "I need you to be calm. And ready."

"Ready for what?" Her voice shook. She was on the verge of hysteria.

"Behind your seat is a length of rope and a harness. Grab them."

As they bumped along the rocky and rutted path just barely wide enough for the truck, she forced herself to reach behind her seat, tugging out the length of coiled rope and a thick black harness. "I have them both. Why do you have these in your truck?" Though she had no idea how these would help them evade their pursuers. Rock climbing was not something she could do.

A spray of bullets hit the back of the truck, the cacophony of noise echoing through her head. Her heart rate jumped with terror. "They're shooting at us!"

A loud pop reverberated through the truck. The back end fishtailed. Chase slammed on the brakes and brought the truck to an abrupt halt. "The tire's blown." He yanked open the glove box and pulled out his gun. "Let's go!"

Frantic, she scrambled out of the truck. Chase took the rope from her and grabbed her hand, pulling her into the trees.

"This way." Chase led her deep into the thick forest.

"How can this be happening?" Ashley's legs burned with exertion as she pushed to keep up with Chase. The underbrush scraped at her clothes, snagging on her pant legs. They were running in the opposite direction of the mountain.

"Where are we going?" she asked, her breath coming in spurts.

"Hopefully toward the highway and backup."

Behind them, she could hear the thrashing of their pursuers as they followed them into the forest.

Please, Lord, let us get away. She dug deep for more speed while trying to maintain her balance over the rough terrain.

The setting sun dipped below the mountain peak, casting long shadows through the trees, making the already dim lighting harder to navigate the untraveled ground. Animals scurried beneath the brush. Startled birds squawked and took flight.

Chase skidded to a halt at the edge of a large meadow. Ashley tripped over her own feet as she tried to avoid ramming into him. He caught her by the elbow and drew her behind a tree trunk. The last of the sun's golden rays touched the green grass and revealed a grazing herd of

Rocky Mountain elk. Ashley had never seen such large beasts in the wild. Several lifted their heads as if sensing the danger breathing down on them.

"If we go out there, we're sitting ducks," Chase said.

Anxiety squirmed in her chest. "We have to hide." There was nothing but tree trunks in every direction. The men's voices carried on the slight breeze. Fear trembled over her limbs and panic dried her mouth.

Chase's gaze went to the treetops. He stepped away from her with his head tilted upward.

"What are you doing?" Her terrified whisper sounded as loud as a shout in her ears.

He pointed his finger toward the sky. "We have to go up."

Up? No way. Her heart jumped into her throat.

He grabbed her hand again and tugged her forward. They stopped beneath a large ponderosa pine tree. "Here we go."

She followed his gaze to a dark shape about thirty feet from the ground. Dizziness forced her to grab the tree trunk. "I can't climb a tree. I've never climbed a tree in my life."

"There's always a first time for everything."

"You don't understand," she whispered. "I'm afraid of heights."

FIVE

"Are you more afraid of heights than bullets?" Chase didn't wait for Ashley to answer as he wrapped one end of the rope around his waist and secured it to his belt with a belaying device, the mechanical piece of climbing equipment used to control the rope. She was going up into the tree, even if he had to carry her on his back.

"Uh, both." Her voice quaked.

"Bullets will kill you." He held out the harness. "Put it on."

She hesitated.

"Quick," he bit out, needing her to move. Time was of the essence. They had to get up the tree and in place before their pursuers spotted them.

Her hand holding the harness trembled. "What if I fall?"

"You won't. I'll have you. I promise."

Obviously deciding she had no choice but to trust him in this, Ashley hurriedly stepped into the harness. She grabbed onto him for balance, her fingers digging into his biceps as she used him for support. She was clearly still terrified. Unfortunately, there was no time to reassure her more. Once the safety harness was on, he tightened it around her waist as much as possible.

"Now what?" She fairly squeaked the question.

He flung the other end of the rope up and over the lowest hanging branch of the tree and then threaded it through the second belay device attached to the harness. "You climb."

"Shouldn't we keep running?"

"It will be dark soon." He gave the rope a tug, locking it into place on the harness. "If we keep going, we'll risk a twisted ankle or worse."

"What about the flashlight on your phone?"

"Which would be a beacon for the bad guys, revealing our location." He drew her closer to the tree's trunk. Taking her hand, he guided her to the small horizontal slates nailed to the tree trunk. "Feel those. Just like a ladder."

"If you say so." Doubt laced each word.

"You're going to climb up this tree. And when you reach the tree stand—"

"The what?"

Biting back his impatience, he said, "It's a hunters' perch. When we hit the meadow, I figured there had to be one around. It's a perfect spot for elk hunting."

"Is that legal?"

"During elk season." He put his hands on her shoulders. In the waning light, he could barely make out her face but her bright eyes were large and scared. "You can do this. I'll help you."

She took an audible shuddering breath. "Okay." The word came out sounding more like a squawk. "Why don't you go first?"

There wasn't time to soothe her nerves. Didn't she understand? Getting her out of the line of fire was the priority. He could hide, fight or shoot his way out of the forest. But his job was to protect her. If he failed… A deep dread warned he didn't even want to contemplate the thought. He needed to stay focused and trust that God would protect them.

He spun her to face the tree. "Start climbing."

Ashley swallowed back the choking trepidation at climbing the tree in front of her. When she was a child, one of her mother's boyfriends had thrown her up in the air and then failed to catch her. She'd had an issue with heights ever since.

But her life depended on going up this tree. She tilted her head. She could just barely make out the bottom of a hunting platform attached to the tree trunk. It was a long way to the tree stand.

Noise of their assailants making their way through the forest reverberated through the trees and galvanized her into action. She groped the rough bark for the first rung nailed to the tree just above her head and did her best to pull herself up. Her arms shook. There was no way she had the strength to muscle her way up the side of the tree. But then the rope and harness secured around her waist lifted her off her feet. Stifling a yelp, she reached for the next rung.

"Brace your feet against the tree."

Chase's whispered instructions gave her the encouragement she needed to remain calm.

Slowly, she walked her feet up the side of the trunk as she used every muscle she had in her arms to pull herself toward the perch. But she was thankful for the leverage of the rope keeping her stable and adding some lift.

In the distance, another noise, out of place for the forest, filled the air. But Ashley ignored the sound to concentrate on climbing. A cold sweat broke out on her body. Her breathing came out in little puffs.

Finally, she managed to land one foot on the little ledge of wood. From there, it was easier to make the climb, grasping each rung with her hands and pushing with her feet until she was able to grasp the metal edge of the tree stand. Awkwardly, she maneuvered herself over until her feet found stability on a piece of protruding metal with crisscross beams.

There was barely enough light to make out a cushioned seat fastened to the tree and the footrest on which she now stood. She made the mistake of glancing down and nearly passed out. The ground was a long way away.

The rope around her waist went slack as Chase made the climb up. Within seconds, he was squeezing in beside her.

"Breathe," Chase whispered close to her ear.

Inhaling and exhaling, she lifted her gaze and searched for his blue-green eyes in the dim light. Staring at him gave her the courage not to disintegrate into a quivering mess.

Balancing himself precariously on the footrest, Chase whispered, "We need to be as quiet as possible. Be very still. Let's pray they aren't smart enough to look up."

A moment later, the two men hounding them burst from the woods and into the meadow five feet from where Ashley clung to Chase in the tree. The last of the sun's rays glinted off the guns held in their hands, sending a shiver of dread along her spine. Chase drew her just a little closer. The warmth of his reassurance flowed through her.

The two men conferred with each other, then split up, one heading away from Ashley and Chase, while the other one moved in their direction.

Ashley buried her face into Chase's chest and held her breath as the big goon walked right beneath them. *Lord, please don't let him look up.*

The sound she'd heard earlier grew louder, shuddering through the trees.

Chase's arms tightened a fraction more around her. "Yes," he breathed out in obvious relief, his voice barely audible in her ear over the roar. "So grateful for Ian Delaney."

Wind whipped by the helicopter's rotors threatened to fling them off their perch. The flying craft passed over the forest twice above their heads and then hovered in the middle of the meadow before slowly landing.

Their pursuers doubled back, running toward where they'd left their car.

The helicopter's door opened. Kaitlyn and Alex jumped out, dressed in full tactical gear with rifles raised. They hurried toward the trees.

"That's our ride," Chase said. "I don't want my coworkers to mistake you or me for the bad guys." He pressed the app button on his phone, dispelling the darkness around them.

"What are you doing?" Hadn't he said it was too dangerous to use the light function?

"Flashing out the Morse code for SOS."

She supposed it was normal for a law enforcement officer to know Morse code.

An answering flash of light came from Alex. Chase let out an audible breath before he said, "I'll go first. Hang tight."

Chase nimbly descended the tree trunk. Clearly, he was an expert climber. He gave the rope a shake, letting her know it was time for her to begin her climb down. She prayed going down would be easier and less scary than going up.

Keeping her gaze on the tree, she made the

arduous descent and was grateful when her feet hit solid ground.

Unhooking the rope from Ashley, Chase gathered the thick length in one hand and grabbed her hand with the other. "Come on."

They ran toward the helicopter as the wind stirred through her short hair and caused the tall grass to slap against her shins. Every step that brought her closer to the flying craft sent more anxiety twisting through her.

Kaitlyn waved for them to hurry while Alex flanked them, watching their backs. Chase helped Ashley inside the open bay of the large dark blue helicopter. It took all her courage to settle herself inside the space, knowing it would leave the ground. And go up and up. Her stomach hurt and nausea rose to burn her throat.

A small overhead light illuminated the interior of the helicopter. She scooted onto one of the beige bucket seats facing forward, her limbs shaking. Ashley recognized the very good-looking Delaney brothers in the pilot and copilot seats. She'd seen them a handful of times in town.

Chase climbed in next and took the seat opposite her. Dropping the rope onto the floor, he leaned forward and threaded his fingers through hers. His mouth moved, but she couldn't hear him over the rumble of the rotors.

Kaitlyn jumped in, taking the seat next to Ashley, while Alex sat beside Chase and shut the door.

Ashley shuddered with dread. Panic roared in her ears as the bird took off, lifting effortlessly into the air. She scrunched her eyes closed, afraid to see how far above the ground they had flown. Her lungs constricted. She would start hyperventilating at any moment. Chase squeezed her hands until she peeked at him.

With his free hand, he used his index and middle fingers, pointing them at her, then at his eyes, his meaning clear. Keep her gaze on him, not on the fact that they were flying high in the sky.

Swallowing the anxiety clawing up her throat, she nodded. It was no hardship to stare into his blue eyes. Though as the helicopter banked and then slowly descended onto the roof of the sheriff's station, which now sported a heliport thanks to the Delaney family, her stomach lurched and she clenched her jaw so tight she was surprised a tooth hadn't cracked.

When she stepped out of the helicopter, she'd never been so glad to have her feet on solid concrete. Her nerves were shredded. Fatigue and adrenaline letdown made the act of putting one foot in front of the other seem as if she were wading through thick sand.

She could hardly believe the day she'd had. Assassins and heights.

All she wanted now was to find a nice hot bath and bury her head between the covers of a warm bed. Tomorrow had to be better.

She sent up a prayer of praise. The day could have ended so badly. With Chase hurt or dead. It wasn't fair for her to put him and the whole community of Bristle Township in danger.

She was safe for the moment, but this whole disaster proved the point that she needed to leave town sooner rather than later. Before someone did get hurt.

She settled in a chair beside Chase's desk. A few seconds later, the sheriff and Daniel returned from the mountain with the two assailants in handcuffs. Her attackers glared at her as they were led to a jail cell. She didn't recognize either one. And hoped never to see them again.

"What's their story?" Chase asked Daniel, when the deputy returned to the main area of the station. "Did they say anything useful? Did Maksim Sokolov send them?"

Daniel shook his head. "Only word they've uttered since we grabbed them was *lawyer*."

Chase let out a soft growl of frustration. "What about the guy from this morning? Did we get any information off him?"

Ashley shuddered at the memory of the man who'd dragged her to the edge of the cliff. The man Chase had shot and killed.

"We got an ID on him," Alex said. "Randy Brennan. Has a rap sheet that goes back decades. Mostly breaking and entering in his youth, but then he graduated to armed robbery and assault."

"Known associates?" Chase asked.

"Once we get IDs on these two, we'll see if there's a connection," Daniel said.

"This Randy guy said he was being paid well," Ashley told them.

"No doubt," Chase said. "Money may not buy happiness but it definitely will motivate some people to commit crimes."

She nodded, thinking about their conversation earlier. "What happens now?"

"We need to find you a safe place to lay low." There was fire in Chase's eyes. "The Los Angeles district attorney has a leak in his department. And I'm not entrusting you to their care again."

"How do you know the leak wasn't from your department?" she asked.

Gregor had told her not to trust the police. Yet she had. And twice now she'd been attacked. Was one of the deputies in collusion with Maksim Sokolov?

The hurt on Chase's face dug at her. "I get why you're asking. I haven't done a good job of protecting you. But I trust everyone in this department with my life."

"But you did protect me. You saved my life, twice." Which made the idea of his working with Sokolov ridiculous.

But what of the others?

She didn't know these people, really. She wanted to believe in them, to trust them. Even call them friends. But she wasn't sure she could trust her own judgment. All the more reason she should go back into hiding.

"I'd like to talk to the district attorney," she said.

Chase rubbed a hand over the back of his neck. "That's reasonable. Let's get to it, then." He picked up the phone.

Within moments, he had the Los Angeles district attorney on the line. Chase updated him on the situation. "You need to check your house," Chase said. "You have a mole working for Sokolov."

Ashley could hear the district attorney's deep, angry voice shouting into the receiver. "No way. This is *not* on us. It's on you. You said you could keep her safe."

Guilt flashed in Chase's eyes. Ashley wanted to reach out to reassure him that he'd done nothing wrong, instead she curled her fingers around each other and waited.

"Nobody here even knew what time or what road we were taking out of town except me," Chase countered hotly. "And I certainly didn't alert anybody in Los Angeles."

There was a long silence, then the district attorney said something in a much calmer, lower tone that prevented Ashley from making out his words.

"A video deposition is the best solution," Chase said into the phone. He listened, his lips pressing together. "Really. You're going to quibble over the cost?" He rolled his eyes. "We'll set it up here in the sheriff's station. Tomorrow morning." Chase glanced at her. "He'd like to talk to you."

Ashley's hand trembled when she took the receiver from Chase. "Hello?"

A deep masculine voice came on the line.

"Miss Willis, I understand that you are ready to testify that you saw Maksim Sokolov shoot and kill Detective William Peters."

"Yes, sir, I am." Even though she was quaking in her tennis shoes, she was going to do the right thing this time. She turned her back to Chase. "Sir, it would be better for me if I disappear after my deposition tomorrow."

Chase's gaze burned a hole into the back of her head. But she knew she was right. Even if he was too stubborn to see it.

"No can do. You're in police custody now. Let me talk to the deputy again."

"But, sir—" she said.

"No. Now hand the phone over to Deputy Fredrick."

Frustration beat a steady rhythm behind her eyes as she held the phone out to Chase.

Giving her a censuring scowl, he took the phone. "Mr. Nyburg." Chase listened for a moment, then said, "Yes, I understand."

After Chase hung up, he was still for a moment before meeting her gaze. She couldn't read his expression. Was he angry with her? Disappointed? And why did it matter to her?

She had no answer to that question.

Kaitlyn walked in with Maya Gallo and Leslie Quinn following in her wake.

"Ladies," Chase greeted them.

Ashley held her breath, expecting the women to be upset with her for not telling them who she really was from the beginning.

"Jane! Uh, I mean, Ashley, are you okay?" Grasping Ashley's hand, Maya's brown eyes searched Ashley's face. She was dressed in jeans and a lightweight red sweater. Her dark hair was held back in a clip at the nape of her neck.

"Kaitlyn told us what happened to you today," Leslie added. Tall and slender, dressed in a navy pantsuit with a white crisp blouse, Leslie exuded an intimidating air of sophistication. Clearly, she'd come from the dress shop she managed for her mother.

"I'm fine," Ashley told them, though she couldn't hold back the threat of tears. Why weren't they angry with her?

"I found them outside," Kaitlyn said. "They weren't going to go away until they talked to you."

"Thank you. All of you." Though Ashley wasn't sure what she was really thanking them for. Not ripping her head off with accusations and recriminations? For caring about her when she didn't warrant their concern? "I don't know what to say, except I'm sorry."

Leslie waved a manicured hand. "Please, no apology necessary. And there's no better place for you to be than here." She turned to Chase. "Right?"

He held up his hands with the palms facing out as if surrendering. "I keep trying to tell her that. She wants to leave. To disappear."

All three women turned their gazes to her. Ashley squirmed beneath their incredulous stares.

"No way," Kaitlyn broke the silence. "That would be a huge mistake."

"The sheriff and deputies here are the best." One corner of Maya's mouth lifted. "Of course, I'm biased."

Considering the harrowing experience Maya and her brother, Brady, had had on the mountain when treasure hunters kidnapped them in their quest to find the prize, Ashley didn't doubt that Maya was grateful to the sheriff and the deputies for rescuing them. Plus, Maya and Alex had fallen in love and were to be married this coming summer. A happy ending for them.

Ashley didn't hold out any hope for a happy ending of her own.

"But truly," Maya continued. "Kaitlyn, Alex, Chase, Daniel and the sheriff would never let anything happen to you or to any of us in Bristle County."

"That's good to hear you say," Alex interjected as he walked into the room and came over to his fiancée, putting an arm around her waist and pulling her close.

Maya glanced up at him. "You saved me and Brady and this whole town from those nasty treasure hunters."

Alex grinned at her. "I didn't do it all by myself."

"That's right. We're a team." Daniel, who'd been sitting quietly at his desk while this drama unfolded, rose and joined them.

"I trust these officers with my life," Leslie stated. "And so should you."

"We appreciate your vote of confidence." Daniel addressed Leslie, his eyes sparking with amusement.

Leslie slanted a glance at him. "Don't let it go to your head." Turning her attention back to Ashley, Leslie said, "I know you've been staying with Mrs. Marsh, but it wouldn't be wise for you to go back there. You can stay with me. If fact, I think it would be best for Mrs. Marsh to take a vacation to visit her family in Texas."

"I'll see that she does," Daniel said.

Leslie considered him a moment. "Thank you."

"I'm here to serve," Daniel said.

Leslie's eyebrows drew together. "Right. Okay, then." She shifted her focus to Ashley. "You good with staying at my place?"

Taken aback by Leslie's kind offer, Ashley tucked in her chin. "You would do that for me?"

"Of course."

Her gaze swept over the group. She didn't want to be a burden to them. Or put any of them out. Accepting help didn't come easy. It made her feel vulnerable. "None of you really know me. I've done nothing to deserve your help. In fact, by staying, I'm putting you all in danger."

"That's what people do in a small town," Leslie said. "We watch out for each other."

"You're our friend," Maya said.

Kaitlyn pinned her with a pointed stare. "And we can take the danger."

Ashley turned to Chase. He regarded her with a curious expression on his face that she couldn't interpret.

"You should…could stay at my house," he said.

"No," Ashley protested. "I won't put Lucinda in jeopardy."

"Which is why my place is perfect," Leslie

said. "I live alone, I have a gun and I'm trained in self-defense."

Running his hands through his sandy blond hair, Chase said, "I'll stand guard outside."

Kaitlyn stepped forward. "Not necessary. I'll stay with Leslie and Ashley."

"Me, too." Maya grinned. "I'll send Brady to Alex's." She rubbed her hands together. "It will be a ladies' party."

Alex groaned. "Maya."

She broke away from her fiancé, linking her arm through Ashley's. "It will be fine."

"No way. You and Brady will stay at the ranch with my dad," Alex insisted.

Maya opened her mouth, most likely to protest, but Kaitlyn intervened. "It's better this way. Safer."

"Fine." Maya obviously couldn't argue with logic.

"We'll take turns standing guard," Daniel said.

Ashley shook her head, not liking that everyone was going to so much trouble on her behalf. "You guys…"

"No more arguing," Kaitlyn said in a decisive tone.

"Then let's go," Leslie said, heading for the door.

The sheriff stepped out of his office. "Hold up. I need Ashley and Chase to give their statements before they leave."

"You all go on," Chase said. "I'll bring Ashley over when we're done."

"Sounds like a good plan," Daniel said. "I'll take first watch after seeing to Mrs. Marsh."

"No, I will," Alex said.

The sheriff held up a hand. "You two work it out." He turned to Ashley and Chase. "Shall we?"

Bemused by the way these people were willing to circle around her to provide a protective bubble, Ashley blinked back tears of gratitude.

She wasn't sure why God had seen fit to grace her with such a gift. She prayed, as she followed the sheriff and Chase into the sheriff's office, that none of them would regret their decision to help her.

SIX

"How will you get your truck back?" Ashley asked from the passenger seat of the sheriff's personal vehicle as Chase drove them through Bristle Township. Overhead, the sky was filled with stars and the temperature had dropped.

Noticing Ashley shiver, Chase cranked up the heat. "Tomorrow I'll buy a new tire and have Mack, the local auto mechanic and tow truck operator, bring it back to town."

Chase hoped a new tire was all that would be required. He hadn't taken the time to assess the damage before he and Ashley had fled into the woods.

"I'm really sorry about all of this," she said softly.

He turned off the main road onto the Quinns' gravel driveway. He slowed the sedan and reached to take Ashley's hand. "It's going to all work out."

She gave him a sad smile before turning her gaze to the side window. She didn't believe him. Was it that hard for her to trust? Not that he'd given her much reason to place her faith in him. But he was determined to do everything in his power to keep her safe.

Withdrawing her hand from his, she made a sweeping gesture to the ranch laid out before them. "This is really nice."

An L-shaped main house sat off to the right side of the long gravel road with a large patch of green grass in the front yard. A corral and pasture were to the left of the driveway, along with a barn and smaller house. "Is it all Leslie's?"

"The spread belongs to her parents, but they are off traveling the world," Chase told her. "Her dad had a medical scare a while ago. Leslie returned home from Europe to help her mom and stayed after he recovered. She lives in the guesthouse now."

He pulled the vehicle to a halt next to Kaitlyn's truck in front of the guesthouse, which was more of a one-story cottage.

Ashley popped open the passenger door, grabbing her duffel bag from between her feet. "Thank you, Chase. For everything."

She hopped out before he could respond.

He climbed out and hurried to catch up to her. Placing his hand at the small of her back, he walked her to the door, like they were returning from a date or something. A strange sort of uncertainty and anticipation that he couldn't explain ignited his blood.

When they stopped outside the cottage's closed door, she gazed up at him, her pretty eyes filled with gentle concern. "Please, go home and get some rest. We both need to recover from the day."

Tenderness filled his chest. Here she was lecturing him, when he should have been lecturing her about resting and taking care of herself. She was the civilian, not the one trained to handle stressful situations. But he had to admit, he liked her worrying about him, liked the warm and fuzzy feeling of knowing she cared about his well-being. An unexpected yearning to have her affection and attention gripped him.

"I'm not going anywhere." He skimmed his knuckle down her petal soft cheek. "You shouldn't have had to go through all of this. I'm sorry for what happened."

She put her hand on his chest, creating a warm spot over his heart. "You're taking on unnecessary guilt. Don't do that. You protected me and saved my life. End of story."

He covered her hand, marveling at how she was so generous and compassionate with everyone but herself. "I don't think it will be the end of the story. This Maksim Sokolov is awfully determined."

She glanced away, slipping her hand from beneath his and leaving an ache in its place. "I wish I'd never brought this to your door."

Wishing she wouldn't blame herself, he hooked a finger under her chin and drew her gaze back to him. "Now, *you* don't do that. The thought of you facing this danger alone…" A shudder of dread tripped down his spine. "I want to help you. To protect you."

To kiss you.

The errant thought nearly buckled his knees. His heart pounded in his ears. The vulnerability in her eyes tugged at him.

She seemed to lean toward him as if silently willing him to reassure her. Giving him permission to kiss her?

It would be so easy to close the gap and press his lips to hers. The longing pulsing through his veins was stronger than anything he'd experienced before for any other woman. He was captivated by Ashley in ways that both terrified and thrilled him. Her innate kindness, compassion and bravery were alluring.

But giving in to his yearning and taking advantage of her vulnerable state of mind wouldn't be honorable. He prided himself on always doing the right thing. Now was not the time to make an exception.

Clearing his throat, he took a half step back, putting some much-needed distance between them while he regained his composure. "Daniel and Alex will take turns guarding the ranch's entrance while Kaitlyn and I are here with you and Leslie."

She cocked her head for a moment and a slow smile touched on her pretty lips. "You really are a good guy."

Had his expression given him away? Had she known he'd fought the urge to kiss her? Had she wanted him to? He'd have to be more careful.

He turned to the door and knocked lightly. The door opened immediately to reveal Leslie and Kaitlyn crowding the entryway. Clearly, they'd been hovering, waiting for Ashley.

"Come in," Leslie said to Ashley.

Ashley put her hand on his arm, keeping him from leaving. "We'll be okay. You really don't have to stay."

"It isn't a matter of having to," he replied. He focused on Kaitlyn. "I'm going to walk the perimeter."

He moved back, allowing Ashley to enter the house. He needed a moment alone with God to figure out what he was going to do about his growing attachment and affections for the woman he needed to protect.

Ashley shut the front door with a soft click. The two women stared at her with similar expressions of mirth and anticipation on their faces.

A flush heated Ashley's cheeks. For some reason embarrassment squirmed through her. "What?"

Leslie grinned. She'd changed from her pantsuit into black yoga pants and a deep purple T-shirt, and had pulled her honey blond hair out of its bun to hang loose around her shoulders. "For a minute there, we were hoping…expecting…"

Kaitlyn shook her head, setting her dark blond curls shimmering around her face. She wasn't dressed nearly as casually as the other woman. Kaitlyn wore well-worn jeans and a light green Henley-style, long sleeve shirt with the sleeves pushed to the elbows. Her badge and holster were at her waist. "Chase blew it. We thought for sure he was going to kiss you."

So had Ashley. But then he'd stepped away, dashing her hope. He was a man of integrity. And evidently kissing his star witness wasn't in his wheelhouse. She should have been grateful he'd called a halt when she wouldn't have had the strength. She wanted to kiss him. Wanted to believe she was worthy of his attention, despite knowing it was better this way. It would make leaving easier not to have any sort of romantic attachment to Chase.

But how had the ladies known he had almost kissed her? "Were you two spying on us?"

Leslie's grin widened.

Kaitlyn shrugged, totally unrepentant. "The window is cracked open. We could hear and see everything."

Ashley rolled her eyes. "Okay, you guys, stop. Nothing is happening between Chase and me."

Only problem was she kind of wanted something to happen between them. She wished he had kissed her. A missed opportunity that might not occur again. She sighed inwardly. She knew there could never be anything between her and the handsome deputy. Not only were they from totally different worlds, but he'd made it clear he was happy with the way his life was now.

Besides, regardless of what the Los Angeles district attorney said about her staying put, at some point she was leaving this town, whether on her own or with an escort to LA. It would be better for everyone if she didn't get too emotionally involved. She was relying on him to keep her safe. But she couldn't give him her heart.

Leslie tucked her arm through Ashley's and drew her to the couch in the living room where she sat beside her. "I want to know all about you."

Kaitlyn moved to the window and looked out before securing the latch and making sure the curtains were completely closed. Was she expecting something to happen tonight? Chase was out there. Would he be safe?

As her heart rate ticked up, Ashley asked the female deputy, "Alex will be close by, right?"

"I think Daniel is taking first watch," Leslie stated.

"That's right," Kaitlyn confirmed. "And you'll have me and Chase here in case anyone gets by Daniel."

Sinking deeper into the cushions, Ashley asked, "Where will Daniel station himself?"

"At the entrance to the driveway." Kaitlyn perched herself on the arm of the couch. "You don't have to worry. You're safe."

Taking a deep breath, Ashley tried to calm her racing heart. She had to trust these people, but she wanted to think about something other than the danger she was in. Curious about the people she'd surrounded herself with, Ashley met Leslie's gaze. "So…you and Daniel? You two have history, I take it."

Leslie curled her lip. "Yes, there is history. We practically grew up together. His family's ranch borders ours. And with our last names of Q and R, we were always table mates in school."

"And you dated," Kaitlyn interjected.

Leslie rolled her eyes. "You can't call attending one homecoming event dating. And we only went because our parents insisted, but he was a jerk then and he's a jerk now."

Ashley frowned. "Daniel doesn't come across as a jerk." But she couldn't speak to what he'd been like in high school.

Leslie waved Ashley off. "Enough about me. I want your story. Where did you grow up? How did you end up in Bristle Township and why is somebody trying to kill you? Who—"

Ashley held up a hand and turned to Kaitlyn for help.

"She can't really talk about the case," Kaitlyn said by means of rescue.

"It's not like I'll tell anybody," Leslie said. "You don't trust me?"

"Of course I trust you," Kaitlyn said. "It's just somehow the bad guys seem to know our every move. So if you don't know anything, then you can't slip up. And you can't tell anybody that she's staying here."

Leslie frowned. "Of course not. Although Maya also knows she's here, but I trust her not to say anything, either."

A soft knock on the front door had Ashley's nerves jumping. Kaitlyn strode to the door, her hand on her weapon. She peeked through the peephole, then relaxed and opened the door for Chase to enter.

Overwhelmed by how relieved she was to see him, Ashley rose. She needed some distance and rest. "I am exhausted. I promise I'll fill you all in on my past some other time."

Leslie stood and gestured toward the hall. "I'll show you where you're sleeping."

With a nod and smile to Chase, Ashley followed Leslie to a large bedroom. "Is this your room? I can't put you out of your own bed."

Leslie waved away her protest. "Nonsense. You need sleep. We'll camp in the living room." She gestured to a door. "Restroom's in there. Towels under the sink. We'll see you in the morning."

After Leslie left, Ashley showered and dressed in long flannel pants and a matching shirt that she'd purchased at Leslie's store for Christmas. Turning out the light, she prayed and then tried to sleep but her mind raced with nervous energy.

Finally, sometime after midnight, she couldn't take her sleeplessness anymore and padded out to the living room to find Leslie painting her toenails, Kaitlyn watching the news with the sound turned off and Chase sitting at the dining room table with a laptop open. His expression went from grim to commiserating when he lifted his gaze to her. "Can't sleep?"

Ashley shook her head. "I'm too nervous about tomorrow. Mind if I get a glass of water?"

"Help yourself," Leslie called out. "Glasses are in the cupboard next to the sink. There's filtered water in the refrigerator door."

"Thanks." Ashley went to the kitchen, found a short glass in the cupboard and rinsed it at the sink. Having grown up in the Mojave Desert, she'd formed the habit of always rinsing her utensils and drinking cups to wash away the dust. As she turned off the faucet, movement in the window above the sink caught her eye. Unlike the front window, there were no curtains or blinds for Kaitlyn to close. Ashley frowned, going on tiptoe to peer out.

A dark figure appeared in the window. Only the whites of the person's eyes were visible in the ambient light.

Startled, she screamed and she dropped the glass she held as she ducked to a crouch. The sound of glass shattering in the sink echoed through the house and assaulted her ears.

Chase and Kaitlyn ran into the kitchen. "What is it?"

Recovering from her fright, Ashley realized she'd dropped the glass into the metal sink and thankfully not on the floor. Cautiously, she rose and pointed at the window. "There was someone out there."

Kaitlyn grasped Ashley's bicep and pulled her into the living room. "Leslie, take Ashley into the bathroom and lock the door."

Leslie was already moving with her phone in her hand. "I'll call Daniel."

Chase had his weapon drawn. "Stay here," he said to Kaitlyn. "Don't let anyone in."

Kaitlyn nodded, her gun at the ready. "Be careful."

Ashley's heart tore as Chase disappeared out the back door in pursuit of the intruder. Then Leslie was tugging her into the bathroom.

Sinking to the floor, the heavy weight of distress spread through her body. She'd put these people in danger by staying here. She sent up a plea to God to keep them safe.

As Chase's eyes adjusted to the dark, he searched for the prowler. The dark shadows made his quest difficult. Bushes lined the sidewall, providing numerous places of concealment. His nerves stretched tight with readiness. Cautiously, he stalked forward, wishing he'd grabbed a flashlight. He wanted—no, needed—to find this intruder.

A wisp of noise on his left provided a split-second warning. He spun, bringing his gun up just as something metal crashed down on his right forearm. Pain exploded through his system and his hand went limp, his gun falling to the ground.

A person dressed all in black rushed at him. Calling on his one year of high school football as a defensive guard, Chase dropped his shoulder and met the assailant's charge, taking him off his feet and propelling him backward onto the ground with an audible thud.

A siren rent the air, signaling that Daniel was arriving.

Before Chase could secure his attacker, the man rolled to his side, got his feet beneath him and bolted, running away from the cottage toward the pasture that stretched for acres in darkness.

Breathing hard, Chase picked up his weapon with his nondominant hand and contemplated firing after the suspect but he couldn't see the target. Awkwardly, he returned his weapon to its holster, then massaged his forearm where he'd sustained the blow. No doubt the tire iron lying on the ground had been the assailant's choice of weapon.

A moment later, a Sheriff's Department cruiser pulled to a stop and Daniel jumped out.

"What's going on?" he asked, as he raced to Chase's side. "Leslie said there was an intruder."

"One perpetrator. He got away," Chase said and recounted the incident.

"No way could we have anticipated an attacker coming at the house through the field in the dark," Daniel stated.

Logically, Chase agreed that he and the other deputies couldn't have secured all access points of the hundred-plus acre spread. But it made him so mad that the men hunting Ashley had even known she was here at the Quinn ranch. It was like Maksim Sokolov had eyes and ears everywhere. And everything Chase had read online about Maksim Sokolov had chilled Chase's bones.

The guy was a ruthless gangster with ties not only to Eastern Europe but to the Colombian cartel. His name was associated with gunrunning, drug smuggling, prostitution and murder.

And he always managed to evade the law.

Chase remembered Ashley saying that Gregor, the man who'd helped her disappear, had told her not to trust the police because Sokolov owned many of them. Anger burned in Chase's chest. That an officer of the law, who'd sworn an oath to protect and serve, would join forces with the likes of someone like Sokolov made Chase's blood run cold. Dirty cops were a blight on all law enforcement agencies.

He trusted his fellow deputies and the sheriff. He was confident none would reveal Ashley's location. Not intentionally.

But clearly Sokolov had spies in town. And Ashley wouldn't be safe until the man was locked away for good.

Daniel eyed him. "You okay?"

"My ego is more bruised than I am." Keeping his arm tight against his middle, Chase headed back inside, informing Kaitlyn of the escaped intruder.

"You chased him away," she said. "That's a win in my book."

He grunted his disagreement.

Kaitlyn went down the hall and returned a moment later with Leslie and Ashley following close behind.

Chase's gaze collided with Ashley's. Her eyes lit up, sending a ribbon of affection unfurling through his system. In three long strides, he met her halfway. Silently, she slipped her arms around his waist, resting her cheek against his chest.

"The intruder's gone," he told her. The relief that she was unharmed heated his core, lessening the throbbing pain in his injured arm.

Ignoring the curious stares of the others in the room, Chase tucked Ashley's head beneath his chin and held her tight with his left arm. It felt good and right to hold her close. Part of his brain protested, claiming he was digging himself a hole he might not be able to get back out of. The other part of his brain, the one that acknowledged he cared for Ashley, had him placing both arms around her, despite the pain in his right forearm.

She drew back to stare into his face. Her eyes were red-rimmed and her expression troubled. "I was so scared for you."

Her concern touched him deeply. "I failed to capture him."

"He didn't succeed in his plans," she countered, gripping his right arm.

Her fingers dug into what promised to be a deep bruise and caused him to draw in a sharp breath.

Gasping, she quickly disengaged and stepped farther away from him. "You're hurt!"

He flexed his fingers and moved his wrist. "Only superficially."

Wrapping her arms around her middle, her voice dropped to a low whisper. "He's going to keep sending men to kill me."

"We'll deal with them," he assured her.

Pressing her lips together as if to prevent herself from saying something, she only nodded. But he could tell she wasn't convinced. Only time would prove his words true.

SEVEN

The next morning, after stopping by Chase's house for him to change into a fresh uniform, and rubbing some arnica cream that Lucinda had given him on the black-and-blue area of his forearm, Chase hustled Ashley into the conference room of the sheriff's station. A TV monitor had been hooked to a laptop and sat facing a lone chair.

Though her insides still quaked with worry, she'd recovered enough from the ordeal of the night before to find her composure. As long as she didn't let her mind dwell on the fact that Chase had been injured protecting her. Today she'd chosen to wear a pretty blue top borrowed from Leslie over her one good black pencil skirt and low heels. She'd tamed her hair a bit with a hair product she'd found in Leslie's bathroom that smelled of vanilla, a scent that gave her some comfort.

Daniel, wearing the same brown uniform that matched Chase's, was at the laptop. His head lifted as they entered. "Everything is all set on this end." He gestured for her to take a seat. "The sheriff will be in momentarily. He's on the phone with the district attorney in Los Angeles now. When they're ready, I'll conference in the DA. He'll appear on the screen to talk to you."

Daniel left the room as Ashley nodded and sank onto the chair in front of the monitor. She swallowed back the trepidation working its way up her throat. Nerves from the thought of giving her statement to the district attorney had her heart pumping with enough adrenaline to keep the fatigue from a sleepless night at bay.

Ashley, along with Chase, Kaitlyn and Leslie, had stayed up the rest of the night, finally resorting to playing board games to pass the time. He'd sat with an ice pack on his arm in hopes of reducing the swelling and bruising. And every time she'd looked at him, she wanted to cry but stifled the urge.

Now she couldn't wait to get this deposition over with, so she could figure out what to do about the rest of her life and how best to keep anyone else from getting hurt. Once her story became public knowledge, there would be reporters hounding her. Not to mention the ever-present threat that one of Maksim Sokolov's goons would manage to silence her before the trial.

She had no illusions that giving her statement would make her safe. Actually, she believed the opposite.

But she would keep her word to Chase and tell the authorities what she'd seen.

Chase stood at her side and placed a hand on her shoulder. His touch gentle and reassuring. "You're going to do just fine."

She hoped so.

A handsome stranger wearing a pinstripe suit with a red tie walked into the conference room. Of medium height with highlighted blond hair and piercing blue eyes, he surveyed them for a moment, pressing his lips together in apparent disapproval before striding toward Ashley.

Unnerved, she leaned closer to Chase.

"What are you doing here, Grayson?" Chase asked.

"The sheriff called to ask if I would represent Miss Willis," the man said. He shook Ashley's hand. "Donald Grayson."

Panic flooded Ashley's system. Was he here because she'd left the scene of the crime? Her gaze jerked to Chase as she extracted her hand. "Why do I need a lawyer?"

"You're not in trouble," Chase assured her. He turned his questioning gaze to the man named Grayson. "Isn't that correct?"

Mr. Grayson nodded as he set a briefcase down on the conference table. "Miss Willis, you're being deposed and this is a legal matter. The sheriff thought it would be good for you to have some preparation and, if the need arises, representation."

"That makes sense," Chase stated. He smiled at her encouragingly. "He's here to help."

Mr. Grayson sat down at the conference table and opened his briefcase. "I've read your statement. But there are a few things we need to go over in preparation for this deposition." He glanced up at Chase. "My client and I need a moment alone."

"I'd rather stay." Chase angled toward Ashley. "If that's okay with you?"

Uncertainty gripped Ashley as her gaze bounced between the two men. Finally, she decided she had nothing to hide from Chase. "I'd like Deputy Fredrick to stay, please. He's promised to be with me through this whole thing."

Mr. Grayson arched an eyebrow. "If you're sure."

"I am."

"Then let's get started." Mr. Grayson pulled out a notepad. "First off, tell the truth. I know that seems like a ridiculous thing to say but it needs to be said."

Wincing with guilt for having deceived everyone with her false identity, she nodded. "The truth and nothing but."

Mr. Grayson smiled but it didn't reach his eyes. Though they were blue like the handsome deputy's, Chase's were warm and inviting, whereas Mr. Grayson's were like a storm about to hit land.

"Also," Mr. Grayson continued, "I want you to refrain from volunteering information. If you are asked a question and you can answer yes or no definitively, do so. If you don't know the answer to the question, say I'm not sure or I don't know. You can ask to have the question repeated. Take a moment to think before you answer. And I want you to refrain from arguing. Answer only the questions that are directly asked of you."

A knot formed in her tummy as she absorbed his instructions. That was a lot to remember.

"I understand that Mr. Sokolov's attorney will also question you," Mr. Grayson said.

A stab of dread impaled Ashley. She thought she might be sick. "I didn't know that." Ashley turned her gaze to Chase. "Did you?"

"I wasn't sure," he said in a strained tone.

Anxiety spread through her chest. "You should've warned me."

"Actually," Mr. Grayson said. "You're not allowed to have any coaching from law enforcement. Only from your lawyer. Which is why I find it highly irregular to have Deputy Fredrick here."

"I'll be quiet," he said.

Grayson shook his head, clearly deciding that wouldn't do. "I think it's better for my client if you leave. We wouldn't want any suggestion of impropriety on the side of the defense."

Daniel poked his head through the doorway. "The video will be up and running in ten minutes."

"I need to prep my client," Mr. Grayson stated.

Chase took her hand and gave it a gentle squeeze. "He's right. I should go."

Disliking the sting of abandonment stealing over her, she clung to him for a moment.

Dredging up strength from someplace deep inside, she released his hand. She needed to be brave for what was to come and to stand on her own two feet. "I understand."

There was no mistaking the reluctance on Chase's face as he left the room. Ashley stared at the table, willing herself not to tear up. Her throat worked and her insides quaked. Why did she feel so alone when Chase wasn't close by?

"Okay, then," Mr. Grayson said, drawing her focus back to the matter at hand. After walking her through the process of how to answer questions directed at her from the district attorney and the defense council, he slid a piece of paper in front of her with a long list of questions. Her stomach dropped, thinking she was going to have to answer each one.

"The district attorney will ask you some basic background questions," Mr. Grayson explained. "These are the most commonly asked questions. Take a moment to read through them and think about your answers. Be ready to respond if one is asked. I will let the sheriff know we are ready."

"Wait, that's it?" She didn't feel prepared at all. In fact, reading the long list of questions that might be asked, she grew flushed with anxiety. Some of the answers would be embarrassing. Like revealing her lack of education or her lack of family.

"Just tell the truth, Miss Willis." Mr. Grayson rose and walked toward the door. "I promise you everything will be okay."

She didn't take stock in promises anymore.

Staring at the paper in her hands, she decided the questions were pretty simple with simple answers. Her life until the night she witnessed Maksim Sokolov kill a man had been unremarkable in the grand scheme of things. Sure, she'd grown up on the wrong side of town, in a trailer near a refuse container, with a single mom whose desire to be a parent waxed and waned. Ashley had survived and had started to make a life for herself. One day, she hoped to again.

A few minutes later, the sheriff, Mr. Grayson, Chase and a pretty redheaded woman walked in. The woman went to the video monitor. Ashley remembered seeing her around town. But she didn't know her name.

Chase put his hand on her shoulder. "Ashley, this is Hannah Nelson. She is our crime tech specialist. She's going to run the camera and video feed. Daniel had to go out on a call."

Hannah waved at her. "Just call me the jack-of-all trades." She smiled kindly. "Maya and

Leslie and Kaitlyn all said to keep your chin up. They're rooting for you."

Hannah's words filled Ashley with warmth. It was good to know that these people had her back. She really wanted to trust them. There was a cold part of her that doubted any of them could promise her safety from Maksim Sokolov's reach.

"Okay," Hannah said. "We are live in one, two, three." She flipped a switch and a man appeared on the monitor. Clean-shaven, graying at the temples with steel-gray eyes, the man regarded Ashley grimly. "Hello, Ashley Willis, I am District Attorney Evan Nyburg."

Unsure if she should say a greeting back, she looked at Chase. He gave her a slight nod. She turned back to the monitor. "Hello. Can you hear me?"

"I can hear you just fine," Nyburg said. He introduced his assistant, Sarah Miller, and the defense attorney, Amos Henderson. "All right. Let's get this started."

For the next hour and a half, Ashley answered question after question. The district attorney and the defense attorney grilled her to the point that she wanted to scream. But she did as Mr. Grayson had instructed and kept to short, simple answers. She took her time, she thought about her responses and she stuck to only what she knew. She did not elaborate and she did not guess. Her palms grew sweaty and the muscles in her neck knotted with tension but she maintained her composure much better than she'd anticipated.

"I have everything I need," Nyburg stated with a satisfied nod. "We will be issuing a warrant for the arrest of Maksim Sokolov."

"And he will be out on bail within the hour," the defense attorney said. "Your witness is unreliable and will not hold up in court."

Ashley's fingers curled in her lap. Her heart rate tripled. What had she done wrong?

"We'll see about that," Nyburg bit out. "There isn't a judge in the state who will let Sokolov go free. I'll make sure of it." The monitor went blank.

Ashley slumped in her chair. "Is what the defense attorney said true? Am I an unreliable witness? Will Mr. Sokolov not go to jail?"

Chase came over and helped her to her feet. "He was posturing. You did really well. The district attorney will do everything in his power to take Sokolov off the street."

"Indeed, you did well, Miss Willis," Mr. Grayson said with an approving smile that enhanced his good looks. He handed her his card.

"If you need anything, call me. I understand you're staying with Leslie Quinn?"

Taking the card, she said, "Thank you. And yes, I am."

But not for long. Now that this part was over. It was time for her to leave. Tonight. If Mr. Sokolov had wanted her dead before, he surely would double his efforts now.

Somehow she had to go into hiding again. It was for everyone's sake. With her gone, the danger that she'd brought to Bristle Township would also leave. Chase and the others would be safe. Her heart hurt at the thought of leaving, but she had to do what was right and best for them all.

He escorted her from the conference room with his hand at the small of her back. His touch was solid and warm and reassuring. She wanted to curl into him for strength.

"I don't think you should go back to Leslie's," he said, his voice dropping low.

Surprise washed over her. Though she agreed, she hadn't expected Chase to come to the same conclusion, that it was time for her to disappear again. But somehow she doubted that was what Chase had in mind. "Why not?"

He paused at his desk. "We can't take any

chances that Lucca Chinn or anyone else won't leak your location."

A shiver of fear worked over her limbs. "Then I should disappear."

Would Chase help her? Hope spurted through her heart, stirring the affection she'd been trying hard to repress.

"Yes, in a way." He guided her into the sheriff's office.

The sheriff sat at his desk. His silver hair showed signs of him running his fingers through the thick strands, something he did when he was stressed. "Everything is all arranged."

"What's going on?" Ashley didn't like this out-of-control, vulnerable apprehension steeling over her. Decisions for her life were being made without her input. She breathed deep, trying to let go of the need to have some semblance of control.

"You'll stay at the sheriff's house tonight until we can come up with a long-term plan," Chase said.

Startled, Ashley stared at the sheriff. "Oh, sir, I couldn't intrude on you."

"No intrusion," Sheriff Ryder said. "My wife will enjoy female company. And Chase will be on-site for extra protection."

"That's right," Chase agreed. He captured her gaze and the intensity in his eyes held her enthralled. "I'm not letting you out of my sight."

His words and the situation landed like a rock in the pit of her stomach. There was no way she'd be able to slip away and disappear with both the sheriff and Chase watching her every move. Now what would she do? Panic crept in. Staying was dangerous for everyone. And leaving had just become more complicated, if not impossible.

Chase touched her arm. Concern darkened his blue eyes. "Don't worry. I'll protect you with my life."

Didn't he understand? That was exactly what she feared most.

It was bad enough to suspect that Gregor's death was because of her. The guilt was nearly paralyzing. If anything happened to Chase... she didn't think she could live with the blame.

Sunlight broke over the horizon, casting long shadows over the mountain. The creeping sensation of darkness that was at odds with the light of day worked over Chase as he sat at the sheriff's kitchen table drinking coffee, winding his nerves tight. He was thankful for fresh clothes, jeans and a chambray shirt that Lucinda had bought him a few Christmases ago. He had his holster on and his badge.

Sheriff Ryder and his wife had already had their breakfast and started their day. The sheriff had headed to town while Mrs. Ryder went to her Bible study, leaving Chase to wait for Ashley to awaken.

He was glad she was sleeping in. He could only imagine the stress she was experiencing. Living under the constant threat of danger and exposure had to wear on a person. Especially someone as sensitive and compassionate as Ashley. He admired her fortitude. She hadn't crumbled yet. In fact, she'd done so well during her deposition, if he hadn't known how nervous she was, he'd never have guessed. She'd been poised and forthright. He was proud of her.

Despite assuring her that the district attorney wouldn't have any trouble putting Sokolov behind bars, Chase understood Ashley would have to enter witness protection, commonly referred to as WITSEC. The sheriff had already reached out to the US Marshals Service and arrangements were being made.

But until they could put her in the program, it was up to Chase and the Bristle County

Sheriff's Department to protect her. As they would, regardless. But she'd become important to them. She belonged to the community. And it pained him to know she would leave them all behind. He'd have no way to keep in touch. For both of their sakes.

The sound of his cell phone ringing broke the early morning silence. He grabbed his phone from his pocket, hoping the noise hadn't disturbed Ashley. The call was coming from the sheriff's station.

"Chase here," he said into the device.

"I have some bad news." Sheriff Ryder's voice was grim.

Chase's stomach plummeted. He braced himself. "What's happened?"

"The district attorney's office had a break in last night," Ryder said. "Ashley's deposition was destroyed."

"How could that happen?" Chase fought a wave of confusion. "Surely they had security procedures to safeguard against a situation like this."

"One would think," Sheriff Ryder said. "Unfortunately, Maksim Sokolov has been released."

The crime boss had been arrested late yesterday afternoon on the strength of Ashley's testimony. And now he was out!

"What!?" Chase ran a hand through his hair in aggravation and dread. "We have a copy of the deposition. Can't we send it to them?"

"That would be the logical solution, however, the defense has claimed there's no way to ensure that our video hasn't been tampered with."

Gritting his teeth, Chase forced himself to refrain from wishing bad things on the defense. The man had a job to do and despite his poor choice in clientele, the defense lawyer's job was to defend his client, not be logical.

"District Attorney Nyburg is coming to town to depose Ashley in person, but he can't make it today," Ryder said. "Until he arrives tomorrow, we have to be on high alert."

"I need to take Ashley somewhere off the grid." Chase's mind whirled. Where could he take her to keep her safe?

"Agreed. My old hunting cabin would be perfect," the sheriff said.

"Isn't the cabin accessible only by horse or ATV?" He had neither one.

"Yes. Because we don't have ATVs readily available, Kaitlyn has agreed to escort you and Ashley. She'll provide you each with a horse from her family's stock. There's no cell service up there, but you'll have a satellite phone so I can let you know when Nyburg arrives and you can come back down the mountain."

Going to the sheriff's hunting cabin was a sound idea. Chase had been to the rustic dwelling a few times. The place wasn't a five-star hotel but the cots were decent enough. And it was so far off the beaten path there was no way anyone would be able to find them.

"As soon as Ashley wakes, we'll head over for the keys," Chase told him before hanging up.

"Where are we going?" Ashley stood a few feet away, wearing jeans and a lightweight sweater in a pale coral, the hue enhancing the color of her cheeks. Her short platinum hair curled becomingly around her sweet face.

Attraction and affection zoomed through his veins. He wanted to draw her close, tuck her into the shelter of his embrace and keep her safe from the world. This latest development would be a blow. And if he could spare her the distress, he would. But he had to be honest; she deserved to know what had happened, so he told her the disturbing news.

Her face lost its color, making her eyes seem

too large for her face. "Now do you see why I must disappear?"

"Yes. And we're working on it." He told her about the cabin and the district attorney coming to town.

"But what happens after that?" Her voice shook. "Mr. Sokolov isn't going to let me live long enough to testify at his trial. You know that, right?"

He didn't like hearing her say what he knew to be true. Sokolov would do his best to eliminate the threat to his freedom. The man may have a large network of guys willing to do the dirty deed, but Chase was determined to make sure none were successful in their quest.

"You'll enter the witness protection program as soon as possible," he said. His heart hurt to think she'd be taken to some undisclosed location and he'd never see her again. But to keep her safe, he had to let her go. She'd take a piece of his heart with her but that was a small price to pay for her protection. Until then he would do whatever was required to protect her.

Her delicate eyebrows lifted. "So we hide on the *mountain*?"

The way she said the word *mountain*, one would have thought he was saying they were headed to the moon. "Yes."

After waiting a beat for her to digest his answer, her lips pressed together and her eyes hardened as determination settled over her pretty face. "Okay. Let's go." She started to move toward the front door with quick purposeful steps.

He suppressed a smile. She really was a trooper. "Do you want to gather your belongings?"

She spun and gave him a wry glance. "Oops. Yes. I'll grab my bag."

As she headed back toward the guest bedroom where she'd slept, he said, "The place is only accessible by horseback."

She stopped and slowly turned to face him, her eyebrows rising nearly to her hairline. She held up her hands as if to ward off his statement. "I don't know how to ride a horse."

Moving to her side, he said, "I'm a novice as well, but we'll figure it out. Together." He held out his hand.

After a moment of hesitation, she slipped her hand into his, their palms melding against each other. The heat of her touch raced up his arm and wrapped around him. She was placing her trust in him. He prayed he didn't fail her.

EIGHT

Ashley bounced in the saddle as the quarter horse, Othello, hopped over a rut in the trail. She tried to keep her knees loose as Kaitlyn had instructed and not hold on to the saddle horn for dear life, but she was so far from the ground that it was hard not to cling to the horse.

Anxiety twisted in her chest and she kept her gaze straight ahead. Falling wasn't something she wanted to experience, and if she glanced down, she feared she'd find herself hitting the ground face first, and not even her puffy down jacket would soften the fall.

Adjusting her hold on the reins, she shook her head with disbelief at the situation. To evade any more of Sokolov's thugs, they were headed up Eagle Crest Mountain to some remote cabin the sheriff owned. In theory, the idea had merit but in practicality... How had she let herself be talked into riding a horse? This was a new and strange experience.

In front of her, Kaitlyn, wearing well-worn denim and a cinnamon-colored leather barn coat, rode a large black-and-white-spotted horse as if she were one with the animal and saddle. No bouncing, just a nice rolling movement. From what Kaitlyn had shared, the woman had been riding since before she could walk. Ashley tried to emulate her. But she was doing a poor job of it by the way her body was protesting every step the horse took.

Glancing over her shoulder at Chase nearly caused her to slip sideways as a grin fought to escape. He didn't seem to be faring that much better. But at least he'd been on a horse before. He gave her the thumbs-up sign with a cheesy smile as she righted herself. She couldn't help but return his smile with a small laugh.

Riding into the trees through the valley that separated Eagle Crest Mountain and a smaller hill where the Delaney Estate had been built at the top and could be seen in all its glory, she felt freer, albeit sorer, than she had in a very long time.

No one knew where she, Chase and Kaitlyn were or where they were headed, except the sheriff, Daniel and Alex. She had to trust they wouldn't reveal her location. She'd had to do a lot of trusting lately and she felt the stretch of it in her soul. There was no way for Sokolov to send anyone after her out here in the wilds of the forest.

Birds sang in the trees and animals she couldn't see scurried through the underbrush. The horses' hooves made a slight rhythmic thumping sound against the dry ground. She deeply breathed in the pine-scented air, letting the familiar aroma soothe her.

Kaitlyn held up her hand. Assuming she meant for Ashley and her horse to come to a halt, Ashley pulled back on the reins like Kaitlyn had taught her. The pale brown horse stopped so abruptly Ashley almost went headfirst over Othello's neck. Chase's horse bumped up against her horse's rear flank.

"Whoa," Chase said.

She glanced back to see his horse dance a little, turning him in a circle. Relieved her horse wasn't doing the same, she patted the stallion's neck. "Good boy, Othello."

Othello pawed the ground, no doubt anxious to keep moving.

Kaitlyn consulted the map the sheriff had given her with directions to the cabin. She pointed off to the right and led the way into the trees, leaving the hiking path behind.

Holing up in a remote cabin in the woods sounded like an ideal plan. Out of the way, not easy to access and devoid of any way to communicate with the outside world save the satellite phone Chase carried. She doubted her escorts would allow her to stay forever. She didn't want to go back to town. She didn't want to go meet with the DA. She wanted this nightmare to end without any more drama.

But she didn't think that was possible.

The world would keep turning, and she would do what was required of her and go into hiding from a monster with long tentacles. She prayed the US Marshals Service would be able to find her a place far enough and secure enough to be out of reach of Mr. Sokolov.

The sun was high in the sky by the time they reached a clearing where a small single-story building had been erected amid towering pine and evergreen trees. Ten feet away was a wooden corral with a gate. Kaitlyn brought her horse to a halt at the corral and hopped down. She hooked her horse's reins over the top railing, then turned to survey their surroundings.

Ashley's horse automatically came to a halt next to the big spotted horse.

"Give me your reins," Kaitlyn said.

Ashley handed the thin straps of leather over and Kaitlyn wound them around the rail.

Following Kaitlyn's instructions on how to dismount, Ashley attempted to climb off the beast, but her feet got tangled up in the stirrups and she lost her grip on the saddle horn. Panic stole her breath as she fell backward, but then strong hands wrapped around her waist, lifting her away from the saddle and setting her feet on the ground.

The heady scent of man and spicy aftershave filled her senses. It was all she could do not to lean back into Chase's strong chest, wanting his arms to slip around her and hold her fast so that he blocked out the world.

He was doing what he could to help her. That was all she could ask. Wanting anything more from him wasn't wise and would only lead to heartbreak. They both understood her time in Bristle Township was close to an end. Better to put some distance between them or she might give in to her longing for connection and let her heart fall for him.

She stepped away to face him and gave him a grateful smile. "Thank you." Her gaze included Kaitlyn. "For everything."

Above all else, she was thankful because

these two people were willing to give up their own lives for her sake. She'd never had anyone do that and it left her strangely unsettled. She sent up a quick prayer, asking God once again to watch over them. So far he'd answered her prayers.

She didn't want to believe it was just coincidence that had allowed her to survive too many scary situations. Trusting the Lord didn't come easily. Trusting anyone didn't come easily to her.

She'd learned at her mother's hand not to trust in promises or in seeming kindness. However, Chase appeared so sincere. She searched her heart and found that she did trust him with her life. And was aware he would do anything to protect her. Trust him with her heart, she wasn't so sure. But she was learning. Learning not only how to let go of any illusion of control but to appreciate being cared for by others. A hard lesson that pushed and prodded, molding her into a more complete person.

"I'll take the saddles off and give these guys a rub down," Kaitlyn said. "You two take the supplies and get the house situated."

Attached to both of their saddles were packs filled with food, their personal belongings and other necessary items that they would need for their short stay at the cabin.

Chase reached past Ashley and undid the knot holding the packs tied to her horse's saddles. The packs slipped away, and he handed her two lighter weight ones. "I've got the key. I'll be right behind you," he said.

She nodded and made her way slowly across the uneven ground to the weathered front door of the cabin. The place was in need of some tender loving care. Kind of like her. Didn't matter that she was only twenty-eight, she felt ancient. The stress of the last year and a half had taken a toll.

Chase stepped up to unlock and open the door. They stepped into a one-room space. Cots were stacked against one wall. A wood-burning fireplace with a stove stood in the corner. A table with four rickety chairs sat by the window. She bit her lip. "No running water?"

"Nope. Though the facilities are out back." He shrugged and she nearly groaned, picturing herself fumbling around in the dark behind the cabin.

"But there's a stream about fifty yards east. We'll gather some water to boil so that we can use it for washing and cleaning. And we brought bottled water for drinking."

"This is very rustic." Though he'd warned

her, she hadn't expected it to be quite this sparse. "You've stayed here before, right?"

He nodded. "Yes. Quite a different experience from what I was used to." He unpacked food supplies. "It's a bit like stepping back in time to a simpler life. Relaxing in a way."

She figured she could adapt easy enough. "I don't mind roughing it. Beats what is waiting for me in town."

His steady gaze led her to believe that he comprehended what she wanted. His words confirmed it. "We can't stay here, Ashley. Eventually someone would figure it out. We have one night here and then you meet with the district attorney. By then the US Marshals Service should have everything in place."

Why wasn't she as eager as she should be to enter WITSEC? "And then I'll disappear again."

He looked away and busied himself unpacking a second bag. "Yes, you will."

From the tone of his voice, she had the impression he didn't like the idea of her leaving for good any more than she did. Oh, she wanted to disappear, never to be found by Maksim Sokolov, but she didn't want to leave Chase. Despite her best efforts, he'd invaded her heart.

She cared for him in ways that made her uncomfortable and giddy at the same time. But she had to put a pin in her emotions and deflate her growing attachment to the handsome, kind, compassionate and honorable man. Nothing good would come from the fallout of leaving her heart behind when she finally did relocate with a new name and blank slate. "If I'm going to be on my own, away from you, who's going to protect me?"

With a twist of his lips, he heaved a sigh of frustration. "I'm not going to lie to you. You'll be under the care of the US Marshals Service, but they won't be able to provide you round-the-clock protection."

Her heart sank. Once again she'd be alone and vulnerable to attack. There had to be something she could do to protect herself. "Life is so unfair sometimes."

Facing her, he held her gaze. "God never promised fairness, only that He would be with us through all of life's circumstances."

His words slipped inside of her, spreading hope within her like warm butter on toast. She clung to that hope, even though she hadn't been aware of God's presence very often in her life. She had to believe God had kept her alive so far for a reason. Having the confidence that God would continue to sustain her through this nightmare bolstered her courage.

Resolute determination squared her shoulders. "Then I need to learn how to protect myself. I want you to teach me how to physically defend myself against an attack. I need to know what to do if someone tries to grab me again like that fake police officer."

Chase contemplated her request, then nodded. "You know, that's not a bad idea. Between Kaitlyn and me, we could show you enough basic moves so that you could at least incapacitate an assailant long enough to run away. And really that's all you want. Run and hide." His intense gaze bore into her. "Don't think you can ever take on somebody bigger and stronger than you and hope to win."

She bristled. He thought she was weak. Okay, so she wasn't physically strong but it infuriated her to know that he thought it, too.

He made a face and held up a hand. "Before you get upset, I just want to say this has nothing to do with your being a woman. It's simple physics."

"So you would give the same advice to Kaitlyn?"

He thought for a moment. "Yes and no. If

her life depended on it, I would say fight. But she's had years and years of training."

"Not to mention muscles," Ashley muttered.

A smile played at the corners of Chase's mouth. "This is true. And she is a deputy with a gun. But the smart thing for you would be to disable your attacker and then run like the wind. Get as far away as possible and hide or find a public place where you can get help."

That made sense and seemed more doable than single-handedly taking down a bad guy intent on harming her. The thought turned her knees to jelly.

"In fact, I would suggest you should always stay where there's other people," Chase continued. "Going into that dark alley by yourself that night—should never have happened."

"It was my turn to take out the garbage," she protested.

"I'm not saying you did anything wrong by doing your job." He gentled his tone. "The responsibility lies with the person in charge."

"Gregor."

"Yes. He put you in an unsafe situation."

"I get what you're saying." She blew out a breath in an attempt to release the guilt that had sprung up. Gregor may not have thought she was in danger by sending her out with the garbage, but he'd helped her afterward. And it most likely cost him his life. "I have no illusions that a few hours of some basic self-defense will turn me into a black belt or anything. But it would make me feel better if I at least knew how to get away."

The cabin door opened and Kaitlyn walked in. "I just heard the very end of that. What is it that you want to do?"

Chase explained Ashley's request.

Kaitlyn regarded Ashley with an assessing gleam in her blue eyes. "I think a little self-defense clinic is an excellent idea. We can teach you enough to know how to break a nose or crush a foot."

"Namely, hobble an attacker," Chase added.

Kaitlyn grinned. "Yes, and there is one particular move that's my favorite. A blow to the knee does the trick nicely. Let's unpack and then we'll have a lesson."

Giddy anticipation raced through Ashley's blood. Finally, she was doing something proactive, something that would keep her as safe as she could be without her bodyguards watching over her.

They made quick work of unpacking their supplies and arranging the cots for later when they would sleep.

They headed outside and found a patch of cleared ground.

"Okay." Kaitlyn rubbed her hands together. "First off, let's talk about the parts of your body you can use to defend yourself with." She touched her elbows. "You have two very hard pointy objects with which to jab." She drew her bent elbow back. "Strike or ram."

Keeping her elbow bent, she made a sweeping motion that brought her elbow up and around, plowing into an imaginary foe. Then she lifted her other elbow and swung her arm in a downward motion, like a hammer.

Rubbing her own elbows, Ashley could envision the blows would hurt, both the attacker and her.

Kaitlyn then held up her hands and hit the heels of them together. "The heel of the hand is an effective tool for a head shot, too. You'll want to aim for the nose, the ears and under the chin." She motioned to Chase. "Come at me."

Ashley held her breath as Chase faced Kaitlyn and reached for her. Kaitlyn's cocked wrist thrust upward toward Chase's nose, stopping a hair's breadth before contact.

Chase didn't flinch. The man had nerves of steel.

Ashley blew out a breath. "Wow."

"You can also go for a knee or the groin. Grab your attacker by the shoulders, using his body for leverage as you ram your knee into the vulnerable spots." Kaitlyn demonstrated on Chase.

Ashley winced. Hurting someone went against every grain in her body. She'd have to get over it.

Kaitlyn turned around so that her back was to Chase. "If your assailant grabs you from behind, trapping your arms…"

Wordlessly, Chase put his arms around her torso, pinning her arms to her sides.

"Immediately, stagger your stance and bend your knees." She demonstrated. "This will draw your attacker off balance. At the same time twist and pivot from your feet until you can get at an angle." She moved as she spoke and then brought her heel up and touched it to the outside of Chase's knee. "At this point I'd ram my heel here. He'd buckle because knees aren't made to bend from the side."

"Or she could also stomp on her assailant's foot," Chase said, releasing Kaitlyn.

"True. The heel on the instep or a kick to the shin will also be effective."

"Now your turn." Kaitlyn stepped aside.

Ashley's mouth went dry. "I don't think I can do that."

"You can," Chase said. "The other thing you should know is how to break a hold if someone grabs you by the wrist." He reached out and took hold of her arm a few inches above her wrist. "What do you do?"

She tried to move away and jerk her arm free but he held on tight. "Okay, that's not working. What do I do?"

He released her. "You grab my wrist."

She grasped his left arm. He immediately pinned her hand to his arm, stepped toward her and swung the arm she held around in a swift move that put him in control and twisted her arm backward at an awkward angle. Then he pushed her so that she had no choice but to sink to the ground.

"Whoa," she breathed out.

"From here, with your attacker down, you could kick or knee the guy to give you a few more moments to get away." He released her.

Excited by the simple yet effective move, Ashley jumped to her feet. "Teach me that move." She held out her arm for him to grab.

Over and over, she practiced the various self-defense tactics until it grew too dark outside to see. Kaitlyn had left them to work together while she went to the creek for water.

Chase was patient as he repeated moves and instructions, making sure she understood the techniques.

She couldn't have asked for a better instructor. Despite her best effort, she was falling for him. She had to fight it with every fiber of her being, yet the question that kept playing through her mind was, how was she ever going to leave this man?

Chase stared at the darkened ceiling, his hands cradling his head while he lay stretched out on a cot near the door. The ladies were sleeping side by side in the far corner. Every once in a while one of them would move, their cot creaking, the blankets rustling. No doubt Ashley couldn't sleep. They'd spent several hours vigorously training.

His heart was still pumping fast, though he acknowledged it wasn't from the physical activity but from spending extended amounts of time with Ashley. She was so determined and eager to learn. It made his heart ache with dread, knowing she would be gone from his life soon. He wished there was a way she could stay in Bristle Township. But there wasn't.

The best thing for her was to go into the

WITSEC program where she'd have a new identity in an undisclosed location.

He could go with her.

The thought pounded through his head.

No. He had a life in Bristle Township. Friends, Lucinda and a job he enjoyed. He couldn't give that up. His tender emotions for Ashley would fade with time. And if he said it enough to himself, he might one day believe it.

The shrill ring of the satellite phone exploded in the silent cabin. Chase jumped from his cot and hustled to grab the device from his pack.

A flashlight beam illuminated the room as Kaitlyn joined him.

"You got it?" Kaitlyn asked.

"Yep." He lifted the antenna and pressed the button to answer. After a few seconds of silence while the phone connected via satellite, Chase said, "Hello."

"Chase." Daniel's voice came through the line. "We have a problem."

Dread and anxiety crushed Chase's chest. "Tell me."

"I found a listening device attached to the leg of a desk. We believe when the fake Detective Peters was in the station, he planted it."

That was how Sokolov's men had known

where Chase and Ashley were when they'd left for Denver. The ramifications of this disturbing news hit Chase like a hoof to the gut. Sokolov no doubt knew where they were now.

"Uh, Chase," Ashley's voice trembled. She stood at the window. "There's someone outside."

NINE

Chase dropped the satellite phone and vaulted across the room, launching himself at Ashley, tackling her in a full contact embrace and taking her to the ground just as the world erupted in a barrage of gunfire.

Bullets pitted the wooden walls. Glass shattered, raining down on Chase's back. Heart pounding in his ears, he braced himself for the painful impact of a bullet. He would protect Ashley with his body, with his life. He prayed Kaitlyn had found cover.

After a moment that seemed to last forever, the gunfire ceased. The ensuing silence was deafening. Breathing a small sigh of relief to not have a gunshot wound, Chase lifted his head slightly. "Are you okay?" he whispered against Ashley's ear.

"Yes," she squeaked.

He turned his head toward the spot where

Kaitlyn had last stood. Embers in the cast-iron wood stove glowed eerily. "Kaitlyn?"

"I'm here, behind the stove," came her whispered reply. "I let Daniel know we're in trouble."

Appreciating Kaitlyn's quick thinking in picking up the phone he'd dropped and letting Daniel know what was happening, he eased away from Ashley, but he kept his hand on her shoulder to ensure she stayed down. "We're going to crawl as fast as we can to the wood stove. You're going to get behind it."

He didn't wait for her to answer, but prodded her forward. They scrambled across the hardwood floor now littered with glass. The sting from shards of the busted window bit into his skin. When they reached the wood burning stove, he maneuvered Ashley behind it.

"What are we going to do? There's only one way in and out of this cabin." Ashley's panicked question made Chase wince.

"And they know that," Kaitlyn said grimly. "It's only a matter of time before they come in and finish what they started."

"No, we're okay. There is another way out." Chase groped the floor, searching for the lever. "The cabin doesn't have a foundation because we're on government land. The sheriff keeps the firewood under the floor. There's a hatch here somewhere."

"I'll help you search." Ashley's scared whisper brushed against his neck.

"No. Stay put." He didn't want her exposed. "Kaitlyn, are you armed?"

"Yes."

"Keep them busy. If someone comes through that door, shoot him." He placed his hand on his own weapon and unlocked the holster so he'd have easier access.

"Roger that." Kaitlyn moved to the window.

"We only want Ashley Willis," a man's voice shouted from outside the cabin. "Our business isn't with you two deputies. Save yourselves and hand her over."

"Not going to happen," Kaitlyn yelled back. "You better take off or I'll take you down."

Coarse laughter met her threat.

"Keep them talking," Chase said, as he continued searching for the latch to open the trap door in the floor. Sweat rolled down his back from the anticipation of their attackers breaching the cabin before they managed to escape.

"Who sent you?" Kaitlyn called out.

"Doesn't matter," the same man yelled back. "Send out the woman."

"You know we can't do that!" Kaitlyn replied.

Silence met her announcement.

"What are they doing out there?" Ashley asked.

"They're going to wait us out," he said. "Obviously, they're in no hurry. They don't know that we've called for backup." His hand closed over the latch and he eased the hatch open. He lay on the floorboards and reached into the hole to find a large stack of wood. As quickly and silently as possible, he removed the short logs, haphazardly pushing them aside. A slight breeze blew through the opening as he created enough space for them to drop into and crawl out from beneath the cabin.

"Okay, ladies, get ready to move. We'll have to crawl out from beneath the house."

Ashley moved to his side and put her hand on his arm. "We can't go out there. What if they see us?"

"We have to. My priority is getting you to safety. Staying here isn't safe."

"Getting *all* of us to safety," Ashley protested.

"Yes. All of us." He appreciated her concern. "I'll go first, then you and then Kaitlyn."

"And…then what do we do?" she questioned in a whisper.

Good question. "Not sure yet. I'm winging it here."

"If I can make it to the corral and get to the horses, we can escape," Kaitlyn said.

"Assuming they haven't let the horses go," he replied.

"Dancer, Othello and Buttercup won't go far if they have been released," Kaitlyn assured him.

He wished he had as much confidence in the horses' loyalty. But the horses were Kaitlyn's animals and he trusted her to know. "All right. Let's go."

He squeezed through the opening headfirst with his arms out for support. Once he touched the ground, he belly crawled to the edge of the cabin's frame, on the opposite side from where the bullets had come from. When he was assured there was no one around, he shimmied out and gave a slight rap on the wall to let Ashley know it was her turn to crawl out. Crouched down, making himself as small as possible, he heard the faint noise of Ashley's movements.

"Give me your hand," he whispered, reaching out for her.

In the dark, her hand touched his, then held

on as she made her way out from beneath the cabin.

After giving the wall another faint rap, he pulled Ashley behind him so that she was wedged between the cabin and him as they waited for Kaitlyn to join them.

"You two stay put." Kaitlyn's voice, barely discernible, came at him in the dark. "Let me check out the horse situation. If I can set them loose, then you two meet me in the woods behind us."

"Copy," Chase said, the one word barely above a whisper. It was important now that they stay as silent as possible so as not to draw the attention of their attackers.

Kaitlyn moved past him toward the edge of the cabin and then she was gone.

The whinny of the horses alerted Chase that Kaitlyn had reached the corral. He sent up a prayer that the men out front didn't understand the noise was the horses greeting their owner.

"What's got those horses spooked?" one of the men said, his voice carrying on the breeze that had kicked up.

"Maybe a copperhead snake," another man said.

"Oh, man, I hate snakes."

"Pipe down," a third man demanded. "I'm going in."

The sound of boots on the porch shuddered through Chase.

There was a rustling sound and then the pounding of hooves as the horses bolted from the corral, disappearing into the forest.

"What's she doing?" Ashley whispered in his ear.

"Creating a diversion," he whispered back. Kudos to Kaitlyn. The longer she kept the men from breeching the cabin, the more chance they had to get away.

"Hey! Who let the horses out?" one of the men shouted.

Not waiting to find out what the men decided to do, Chase tugged Ashley away from the cabin. "This way," he whispered in her ear.

He tucked Ashley close and together they ran toward the shelter of the trees. They found Kaitlyn behind the trunk of a large Douglas fir.

"We need to reach the creek," Kaitlyn whispered.

"What about the horses?" Ashley asked, also keeping her voice low.

"They'll come running when we're ready for them," Kaitlyn answered.

Shouts of the men galvanized Chase into

action. Their attackers had discovered the empty cabin.

"Lead the way," Chase urged Kaitlyn.

He put Ashley in front of him so he could protect their flank. The going was slow in the dark. He kept a hand on Ashley's shoulder to steady her when she stumbled.

The rush of the creek, swollen from the winter runoff, led the way forward. When they reached the edge of the canopy of trees, the moon shone bright on the rippling water of the creek a few feet away.

Kaitlyn let out a shrill whistle. "It will be a moment or two."

"We should stay near the trees." He didn't like the idea of being exposed out in the open.

They took cover at the base of a tree that had large bushes growing up around it.

"Will the horses be able to find their way in the dark?" Ashley's voice held concern.

"Yes. They have excellent night vision," Kaitlyn replied.

"That's a relief."

Chase smiled to himself at Ashley's innate concern for others, even horses. She was such a caring and generous woman. One of the many things he'd come to admire about her.

"What was Daniel saying to you on the SAT phone?" Kaitlyn asked.

Remembering the disturbing news, a fresh wave of anger coursed through Chase's veins. "He found a listening device in the station house."

Ashley gasped softly. "How did it get there?"

"Only way I can think of is when the fake Peters showed up, he must have planted it," Chase told her.

"That's how they found out we were here." Kaitlyn's tone held a sharp edge. "I figured it had to be something like that. These bozos wouldn't know how to track anybody on their own."

Ashley made an irritated growling noise in her throat. "Mr. Sokolov has known our every move. He's insidious."

Chase slipped his arm around her shoulders. "He won't be privy to any more information on you now."

She leaned into him. "I hope not."

The bobbing of flashlights moving through the trees sent Chase's heart slamming against his rib cage. "They're coming."

Kaitlyn pushed away from the tree she'd been leaning against. "We need to cross to the other side of the creek."

Deciding it was better than waiting to be found, Chase urged Ashley into the knee-high flowing water. Through his shoes and pant legs, cold zapped his flesh to the bone. He kept a firm grip on Ashley's biceps as she sucked in a sharp breath of distress at the icy temperature of the creek.

She slipped, letting out a muted yelp, and he pulled her firmly against him. "Steady now."

"I pray we get out of this alive," she whispered. "And with all our toes."

"We will," he told her and sent a prayer heavenward that he wouldn't be proven a liar. Moving slowly over slippery rocks and against the current's tug, they reached the other side of the creek and hustled to the cover of more trees.

Kaitlyn let out another soft whistle that sounded more like a bird's call. A few moments later, the three horses appeared, their hooves splashing in the water as they ran along the creek. The three horses stepped onto the bank and moved toward their owner with Dancer in the lead.

Kaitlyn held up her hands. "Whoa," she cooed gently.

The three animals slowed to a halt.

"I didn't have time to put their saddles on,"

Kaitlyn told them. "Only their bridles. Not ideal but we'll have to manage."

Chase kept an eye on the light bobbing through the forest. They were getting closer every second. Worry chipped away at his confidence. Urgency sharpened his tone. "We need to go."

"I don't know about this." Ashley's voice was low and uncertain.

"It's not much different than with a saddle," Kaitlyn said. "Grab some of Othello's mane near his withers."

"His what?"

Chase could tell Ashley was on the verge of panic. He didn't blame her. It was one thing to ride while secure in a saddle with stirrups for your feet to help you stay in place. And with no experience riding, he understood her confusion about the animal. He stepped closer. "I'll help you up. The withers are the ridge between the horse's shoulder blades."

"Oh." Ashley reached to grab a handful of Othello's black mane. "Now what?"

"I'll lift and you swing your leg over," Chase said. "Ready?"

She gave an audible gulp before she let out a strained, "Yes."

He put his hands at her waist and lifted her

off the ground. She swung her leg over and settled on the horse's bare back.

Kaitlyn handed her the reins of the bridle that would control the horse's head. "These horses are used to being ridden bareback, but it is challenging. You'll need to sit upright, no slouching or hunching over. Keep your legs draped over the horse. Try not to grip or draw your knees up. The horse is going to feel every movement you make. This is going to challenge your balance."

"Wonderful," Ashley muttered.

Committing Kaitlyn's instructions to memory, Chase hurried to Buttercup.

Kaitlyn moved with him. "Drape your torso over his back and then swing your leg over."

He did as instructed and easily found himself sitting on the horse. It was a very different sensation than with a saddle, and he figured he and Ashley would be sore when this was over.

Kaitlyn easily mounted her horse. "I suggest we head to the Delaney Estate."

"Lead the way, Kaitlyn," Chase said, eager to be gone before the men pursuing them discovered their whereabouts. "You still have the phone, right?" he asked, with hope coloring his voice.

"Of course." She patted the cargo pocket on the thigh of her pants.

"Good. Let Daniel know where we're headed and about the men hunting us."

"On it."

The second Dancer took a step, Othello and Buttercup followed. Kaitlyn led them through the dark forest. Chase barely heard her talking to Daniel on the phone. Chase kept half his attention behind him, praying they'd outsmarted their attackers. The journey toward the safety of the Delaney's rolling mansion at the top of the next rise was harrowing and physically uncomfortable but a small price to pay considering the alternative.

By the time they arrived at the Delaney Estate, Ashley's body hurt. Tension radiated through every fiber of her being. Not only from the anxiety of being pursued through the forest but from sitting on a horse with no saddle. Riding bareback was a strange experience, one she didn't want to repeat anytime soon, but she trusted the horse as Kaitlyn had told her to do and the animal hadn't dumped her off, which was a win. Her core muscles were taut with the constant need to keep her balance atop Othello.

Lights flooded the Delaney property as they halted the horses in front of the large ornate metal gate. Kaitlyn buzzed the intercom.

"State your business," a man's deep voice stated, coming out of the box.

"Tell the Delaneys it's Deputy Kaitlyn Lanz of the Sheriff's Department."

"One moment, please."

Slowly, the gate opened and they rode the horses up the paved drive, past an illuminated manicured lawn and hedges that were trimmed into animal shapes. Ashley had never been here before and had never thought she would have an occasion to visit the Delaneys in all their splendor. The structure reminded her of a castle from a fairytale. She'd heard the elder Delaney was eccentric, the treasure hunt last year being proof of that, but this mansion was so whimsical that she wondered what type of person would create a place like this in the middle of the Colorado forest.

The front door opened and Nick Delaney, the younger of the Delaney brothers, stepped out and hurried down the large staircase, heading straight for Kaitlyn as she drew her horse to a stop. He wore designer jeans and a form fitting long-sleeved T-shirt that accentuated lean muscles. "Well, aren't you a sight for sore eyes."

Ashley's horse came to a halt next to Kaitlyn's, with Chase moving in next to Ashley.

Kaitlyn hopped off Dancer. "Where's Ian?"

Nick shrugged. "Not here. What can *I* do for you?" He grinned and wagged his eyebrows.

"This was a mistake," Kaitlyn stated, half pivoting away as if she were going to remount her horse.

Nick's expression cleared and grew serious beneath the house's outside lights. "Really, what can the Delaneys do for you? We're happy to help."

With a huff that Ashley decided was a mix of exasperation and surprise, Kaitlyn handed him the reins of her horse. "Hold this." She turned away, but said over her shoulder, "Don't let her step on you."

Ashley pressed her lips together to keep from laughing at the way Nick's nose scrunched up as if he'd eaten a lemon.

"Step on me?" He backed away from the horse, stretching the reins out as far as they would go. "Why would the horse step on me?" He eyed the big bay as if afraid the animal might charge him. "Are you a mean horse?"

Chase slipped off his horse and came toward Ashley.

Kaitlin took hold of Othello's bridle. "Okay, Ashley," Kaitlyn said. "You're going to fall into Chase's arms."

Ashley raised her eyebrows at Kaitlyn. "Excuse me?"

Kaitlyn's smile was much too innocent. "I mean, you're going to slide off. Pretty much like before. Grab the reins and some of the mane, lean forward and then swing your right leg over the back of the horse and slide down."

Chase moved closer. "Come on, you can do it. I'll catch you if you fall."

Ashley blew out a breath. Unfortunately, she doubted she'd be graceful. "You better catch me, Chase."

"Don't worry," he said. "Trust me."

He was always saying that, and it hadn't always worked out. "Who are you trying to convince? Me or yourself?"

Moonlight displayed the face he made. "Both."

Tilting her head, she said, "I trust you to catch me if I fall."

"I know I've let you down before," he said. "I—"

"Stop." She cut his words off. "You're human

and not infallible. Evil is evil, sometimes un-stoppable. You can't control all circumstances, no matter how determined you are."

He touched her knee. "You're right. I pray every moment that I'll be enough."

She wanted to tell him he was, but she re-mained silent, knowing if she spoke, she'd re-veal just how enough for her he was. That if she weren't careful, she'd give him her heart.

Holding on as instructed, she leaned for-ward, lifted her right leg and brought it over the horse. Othello chose that moment to move. She lost what little balance she had and plum-meted straight into Chase's strong arms.

He set her gently on the ground. "See, I didn't let you fall."

On impulse, she reached up and kissed his cheek. "No, you didn't and for that I'm grate-ful."

His lopsided grin sent her heart thump-ing. His gaze dropped to her lips. Her pulse jumped. Yearning flooded her system. She wanted him to kiss her. Instinctively, she leaned toward him.

Kaitlyn cleared her throat, disrupting the moment. Ashley jerked back, her cheeks heat-ing. She hoped her blush wasn't visible in the glow of the house lights.

"Let's get inside before those bumbling henchmen decide to find us and climb the fence," Kaitlyn said.

"Hey, wait a second," Nick said. "Henchmen?" He handed Kaitlyn back the reins to her horse. "There will be no henchmen climbing our fence. Follow me."

He led them into the large sprawling mansion. Ashley marveled at the marble floors, sweeping views from the large windows and a wide staircase with a wrought iron railing leading upward to a second floor. Impressive paintings that she'd only seen in books adorned the walls. There was a museum-like quality to the home. Not as whimsical inside as outside.

Nick shut the big oak door behind them with a solid thud. An older man, wearing a black suit with the buttons mismatched as if hastily put on, stepped out from a side door.

"This is Collins, my father's valet and the house butler," Nick said. "If you're hungry, he can fix you something to eat."

They all declined. Ashley couldn't fathom being wealthy enough to have a valet/butler. She wasn't even sure what a valet was, but he seemed like someone only the rich needed.

"Then would you see to their horses," Nick told the man.

"Sir?" Collins's expression was a mixture of confusion and concern.

"Seriously," Nick stated. "They came riding horses. Old West style."

"Very well." Collins headed for the front door. "I will handle them."

"Make yourself at home." Nick waved toward a room to their right. "That's the library. You'll find bottles of water in the mini fridge."

"Do you happen to have any pain reliever?" Ashley asked. Her body was bruised and sore, but thankfully not broken.

Sympathy flashed in Nick's eyes. "Of course. My father keeps a stash in his desk. Top right drawer. Help yourselves. I hope you find some relief." He strode away.

Ashley and Chase moved toward the library and stopped when Kaitlyn didn't move. She stood rooted to her spot, watching the younger Delaney brother disappear down a corridor. "I wonder what he's up to?" Her gaze narrowed. "I'm going to find out." She stalked after Nick.

Ashley wasn't sure what was up between the deputy and their host. But they seemed to be at odds on everything.

Chase shrugged and led the way into the library. Another wall of windows greeted them. Ashley wanted to see the view in the daylight.

A few lights twinkled in the distance. Were they facing town? The other three walls were filled with volumes of books.

A large massive desk sat in the middle of the room. Ashley found three different types of pain relievers. She took two from a bottle. "Chase?" She held up the container.

He nodded. "I'll take two."

Chase went to the mini fridge in the corner, grabbed two bottles of water and handed one to her.

Ashley enjoyed the cool liquid as it washed down the pills. She hadn't known how thirsty she was until she'd drunk nearly the whole bottle. "I never suspected riding horses was so hard."

"We survived," Chase said, finishing off his water and dropping the empty bottle into a garbage can by the built-in bar.

"Yes. But for how long?" The fear that she'd kept at bay while concentrating on staying atop a horse now rushed back to overwhelm her. "What happens when they realize where we've gone and they come after me again?"

"We need to get through the night, then put you in front of the DA tomorrow. The US Marshals Service will take over after you're deposed."

She should have been happy at the news.

This would be the beginning of a new phase. She'd be whisked away to some undisclosed location where Mr. Sokolov couldn't find her. But she wasn't happy. Not in the least. Hiding again—using another fake identity, living a lie—twisted her insides into knots.

She moved to sit in a wingback chair. Sinking into the cushions, she absorbed the softness after the bony hardness of the horse. "I don't know how much more of this I can take."

Chase sat on the little ottoman in front of her. "Listen to me." His intent gaze demanded her attention. "You are doing great. You will survive this. You are a survivor and don't let anyone or anything tell you differently."

She wished she felt like a survivor. But she accepted she was a fraud. And a liability. A nuisance. An albatross around Chase's neck. Leaving with the US Marshals Service would be the best thing for everyone. Only it would be agony on her heart. She sighed. "Thank you. You always seem to know exactly what to say."

He frowned. "If the expression on your face is any indication, I'm not sure if I did more harm than good."

He'd done it again, reading her so well. She rose and stepped away. "No, everything is working out the way it's supposed to. I just have to—" She swallowed hard, her mouth suddenly so dry. "I have to trust that God's in control."

She went to the bookshelves and pretended to read the spines, but her eyes were misty with tears. Strong arms wrapped around her. She hadn't heard Chase move, but for some reason she wasn't surprised that he would offer her comfort, reassurance and his strength. She leaned back into his chest. She'd take it for now.

Because soon they would be separated by confidentiality and distance. The thought of leaving had never hurt so bad.

TEN

The sound of Kaitlyn and Nick Delaney in the entryway of the Delaney mansion heading for the library forced Chase to release Ashley. She hurried away to stand near the floor-to-ceiling window overlooking a dark landscape. His arms were empty and cold without her.

He had to admit, it was better to not give anyone the wrong impression, though. They weren't a couple. No matter how much he liked, respected and cared for Ashley, the paths of their lives were set on different trajectories. There was no intersection where they could travel together toward a mutual future. Part of him wanted to accept the fact and another part wanted to rail against fate. He would do neither.

Grabbing a book from the shelf and pretending interest, Chase looked up as Kaitlyn swaggered into the opulent room with Nick on her heels.

"He armed the fence. Anyone touches it, they'll sustain a nasty shock," Kaitlyn announced as she halted near the desk. "I'm sure it was Ian's doing."

The precautions seemed over the top, but Chase figured with the kind of wealth the Delaneys had, they must also acquire enemies. Last year when the hunt for the Delaney treasure was in full swing, there were many people willing to kill for the prize.

Nick snorted and rested a hip on the edge of the desk. "Why do you assume he's the brains behind our family?"

Kaitlyn's mouth lifted at one corner in a smirk. "I'd be highly surprised to find out otherwise."

He wagged his eyebrows. "Oh, I'm sure I could surprise you in many ways."

She dropped her chin and glared. "Not going to happen."

He cocked his head with a glint in his dark eyes. "I'm not sure what you are inferring, Deputy Lanz."

Kaitlyn's eyes widened, and her mouth opened but no words formed.

Chase almost laughed out loud and his gaze

sought Ashley's. Her lips were pressed together as if she, too, were holding back her amusement at the interplay between the other two.

Kaitlyn finally narrowed her gaze. "When is Ian returning?"

The humor in Nick's eyes dimmed. "Not any time soon. And because my father is with Ian, you're stuck with me as your host. I'm really not that bad of a guy."

Kaitlyn made a face. "I'm going to check in with the sheriff. Then we need to leave." She stalked out of the library.

"I don't think she likes you much," Chase commented.

Nick chuckled and shrugged. "Probably not. But she's much too serious. Just like my brother. But don't get me wrong, I respect anybody willing to put on a badge and do the hard job."

When Nick wasn't doing the adult equivalent of tugging on Kaitlyn's braid, Chase thought he was probably a decent guy.

Ashley moved to stand beside Chase. "We really appreciate you taking us in like this."

"Of course," Nick said. "I'll drive you all into town when you're ready."

"Thank you." Chase itched to clean up. His

clothes smelled of horse and creek water. His socks were still sopping wet inside his shoes. He was sure both of the ladies were eager to get going, as well.

"You have an extensive collection of books," Ashley said.

"My father's passion," Nick said, going on to talk about the rare and first editions that Patrick Delaney had collected over the years. Ashley seemed very interested and for that Chase was glad. Anything to distract them from the danger looming outside the estate's fence. Nick was well spoken and much more conversational when Kaitlyn wasn't present.

Kaitlyn returned, her expression pensive. "I just got off the phone with the sheriff. He'd like us to stay here tonight and come into town in the morning."

"You're welcome to," Nick said. "We have plenty of en suite rooms and Collins can wash and dry your clothing for you."

Kaitlyn stared at him a moment. "Thank you. Your hospitality is appreciated."

Nick nodded but made no comment.

Chase didn't hesitate to take the man up on the offer. At least they would be safe for the night and have clean clothes in which to face the morning.

* * *

"This baby is armor-plated and has bulletproof windows," Nick Delaney proudly explained as he drove the big army green Humvee out the front gate of his estate the next morning.

Nick had insisted on driving them to the sheriff's station, much to Kaitlyn's dismay. Chase's coworker really had an issue with the younger Delaney. Chase wasn't sure what had her dander up. The fact that he was a wealthy man who seemingly didn't take life too seriously or was there something more?

After making arrangements to have the three horses transported back to her family ranch, Kaitlyn had slid into the back seat of the Humvee with Ashley while Chase sat in the front passenger seat. Chase had noticed the glance Nick had thrown Kaitlyn as if he'd been surprised she hadn't insisted on riding up front. To be honest, Chase had been surprised, too.

And though Nick played off his attention to Kaitlyn as bantering, there was no doubt the man was attracted to the female deputy. There was no mistaking the way Nick's gaze followed Kaitlyn when she wasn't watching. The two couldn't be more opposite, and sparks flew when they were together.

Chase, on the other hand, was grateful for the Delaneys' help and their safeguards. Anything to keep Ashley safe. And he refused to analyze why she'd become so important to him.

Today would be a big one for Ashley. Right now the Los Angeles district attorney was waiting at the Bristle Township courthouse. And the sheriff had nudged the US Marshals Service to hasten their timeframe for when they would secure Ashley into the WITSEC program. It was all coming together. So why did Chase's heart sag heavily with something akin to sadness?

As they neared town, the chime of a cell phone rang loud inside the cab. Nick pushed a button on the steering wheel and connected via Bluetooth to the call. "Nick Delaney here."

"Mr. Delaney, this is Sheriff Ryder."

"Hello, Sheriff. I have you on speakerphone with Kaitlyn, Chase and Ashley. We're almost at the courthouse."

"I need you to step on it. I need them at the station right away."

Something in the sheriff's tone sent alarm bells ringing inside Chase's chest. "What's up, boss?"

"We have a situation. I need all of you here. Now." The call ended.

A fist of dread slammed into Chase's gut. What was going on? Was there a problem with the LA district attorney coming to town?

"Well, that was mysterious," Nick said as he maneuvered his way through town and to the end of the main street where the Sheriff's Department sat. The two-story brick building had been repaired and enlarged thanks to the Delaney family after last year's blaze. More specifically, Ian Delaney. The man had expressed his remorse that his father's treasure hunt had fueled the arsonist.

"Pull around back," Kaitlyn instructed.

"As you wish." Nick drove down the side alley into the back parking lot and halted next to one of the official sheriff department vehicles. They piled out and hurried inside.

Chase's throat closed up as his mind registered that the sheriff and Daniel were dressed in tactical gear. Daniel, a former marine recon sniper, held a Barrett M95 manual bolt-action sniper rifle at his side.

Tension bunched Chase's shoulder muscles, but he didn't say anything, waiting for an explanation. Whatever was happening had to be serious. They didn't normally bring out the specialized equipment unless something bad was going down. A band around his chest tightened with anxiety.

Sheriff Ryder pointed to the two chairs off to the side. "Miss Willis and Mr. Delaney, take a seat." There was no arguing with the command. Ashley and Nick settled on the chairs.

"What's going on?" Kaitlyn asked with a frown. She bounced on her toes, a habit that Chase had noticed when his fellow deputy grew anxious.

Before the sheriff could answer, Alex stepped out from another room, also decked out in full body armor complete with riot helmet and two sidearms strapped to each thigh. His grim nod strained Chase's nerves.

"Kaitlyn, we need you to stay here and guard our witness," the sheriff said.

"Against what?" Chase reflexively demanded. He couldn't take not knowing what sort of situation required full-scale assault equipment in their small town. But he had a dreadful foreboding in the pit of his stomach that this had something to do with Maksim Sokolov and Ashley.

The sheriff shifted his attention to Alex and gave a nod.

The empathy in Alex's eyes slammed into Chase. "Lucinda has been taken hostage."

The bottom of Chase's world fell away.

"Oh, no." Ashley's heart sank. She jumped up from the chair and rushed to Chase's side, gripping his arm. "She's in danger because of me."

Alex nodded. "Unfortunately, yes. They are demanding we trade you for her."

Stomach knotting with horror, Ashley stared at Chase. His jaw worked but no words came out. Lucinda was his family. Like a mother to him. The only person he was close to. He had to be devastated. Ashley's chest ached.

"You have to do it," she said despite the terror flooding her veins. "Trade me."

Chase's gaze whipped to meet hers. The dark blue of his eyes turned stormy. "No! Never. Not going to happen. Lucinda wouldn't want that to happen."

"But Chase—" Didn't he understand? She'd do whatever was necessary to ensure Lucinda was released unharmed.

He gave a sharp shake of his head and abruptly turned from her. The dismissal cut deep.

"Where is she?" Chase asked the sheriff.

"She called from her cell phone and Hannah traced the call back to your place," Alex supplied.

For a second Chase was silent, then he nodded. "Okay. We can work with that. Let me gear up." He sprinted out of the room without waiting for permission.

Ashley sank back onto the chair. Fear for Lucinda drained her of oxygen. Her lungs contracted painfully, and panic fluttered in her chest. Ashley remembered what it was like when the man posing as the detective had been about to throw her off the cliff. She hated to think Lucinda was experiencing the same terror. If those men hurt Lucinda, Ashley would never forgive herself.

When Chase returned, he was dressed in a similar fashion as the other deputies. A shudder of alarm worked over her limbs. They were expecting the situation to turn deadly. Why else would they be wearing such intimidating outfits? Nausea roiled through her stomach.

Chase headed for the door. "Let's roll."

"Wait!" Ashley scrambled from her chair. "Take me with you. If worse comes to worst, you trade me. We might as well get this over with. Gregor died for me. I can't let Lucinda pay the ultimate price, too."

Skidding to a halt, Chase whirled to face her. The anger on his handsome face should have scared her but it only made her want to weep with despair.

Chase's voice was hard and unyielding. "No one is going to die at the hands of these thugs. We will rescue Lucinda. You need to remain here."

Aggravated with a potent mix of terror and anguish, she shook her head. He couldn't make that kind of promise. "I can't let them hurt someone else."

She had to do the hard thing and sacrifice her life to save another life. She would not let Lucinda pay the price for her. She bolted for the door. Kaitlyn blocked her path, hands raised.

"Ashley, no."

"But you can use me to draw them out," Ashley argued.

"That won't be necessary," Chase said. A muscle ticked in his jaw. He shook his head and trained his focus on his boss. "There's a root cellar in the basement that has an opening about ten yards from the house. I doubt these LA henchmen of Sokolov's would even know to look for it."

"We can split up," the sheriff said. "Daniel

and I will work from the front of the house while you and Alex go through the back access point."

"What about me?" Kaitlyn asked.

Before the sheriff could respond, Nick stood. "I can keep Ashley safe inside the Humvee."

Kaitlyn turned to him, her expression startled as if she'd forgotten he was there. "You're not a part of this."

He stepped past her to address the sheriff. "I am a part of this community. I can help." He turned to Kaitlyn. "Ian is not the only one with skills. Plus, Ashley will be safest in my vehicle. Being armored and all."

"That's not a bad idea," Alex interjected. "We may need all hands on deck here."

"Gear up, Kaitlyn," the sheriff said, apparently agreeing with Alex. "We'll get the car ready."

Ashley recognized the way Chase's jaw clenched. He wasn't happy with the decision, but the longer they debated, the more likelihood that Lucinda would end up hurt.

Heart pounding in her chest, Ashley hurried out to the Humvee and slid in the back. Chase left with Alex in a separate vehicle. A few moments later, the sheriff drove away with Daniel and Kaitlyn. Nick pulled in behind them and followed them through town toward Chase's house.

Ashley sent a desperate plea heavenward. *Lord, please don't let anything happen to Lucinda. I couldn't take it if she died when I could've done something to save her.* Losing Gregor had been awful, but Lucinda would be worse because of what it would do to Chase.

Chase parked a few blocks away from his house. His heart hammering in his chest and a prayer on his lips for Lucinda's safety, he and Alex hoofed it through Chase's neighbors' backyard to the fence separating the properties. Through the earpiece jammed in his ear, he heard the sheriff trying to negotiate Lucinda's release. Thankfully his boss was keeping the men holding Chase's former nanny hostage busy. Chase and Alex had a better chance of gaining access to the house unseen.

In the shadow of a full maple tree, Chase slipped over the fence and dropped down next to the tree's trunk. Alex joined him a moment later.

Daniel's voice came through the earpiece. "We have two suspects. I have a clean shot."

"No," Chase quickly replied, knowing Daniel could only take out one at a time, which would give the remaining one an opportunity to hurt Lucinda. "We can't take the chance with her life on the line."

"Let us get inside and neutralize them both," Alex said softly into his own headset.

Chase gave his superior a grateful nod.

"Copy," Daniel said.

Lifting a scope to his eye, Chase surveyed the back of the house. He didn't see anyone at the windows or any movement within. What were these goons thinking? What was their plan? How did they intend to escape once they completed their goal of eliminating the threat to Sokolov?

A horrifying thought flittered through his brain and made sweat break out on his neck. Was this a suicide mission? Did they plan to take Ashley out along with themselves and anyone else who got in the way? Could anyone be that loyal to a crime boss? Then again, it probably wasn't loyalty that motivated them, but fear. They likely had families of their own they were protecting.

"We need to be alert for explosives," Chase murmured into his headset.

Alex tapped him on the shoulder once to indicate he heard.

The sheriff's voice came through the ear-piece. "Take care. Godspeed."

Chase lifted another prayer for guidance, then motioned for Alex to follow him. In a low crouch, they moved along the fence line until they were close to the place where the root cellar doors were visible. With another hand gesture, Chase indicated the entrance. Alex tapped his shoulder again one time in acknowledgment.

In tandem, they quickly moved from the fence, across the yard to the metal door. There was a combination lock that Chase quickly undid. He lifted one half of the door and Alex slipped inside the dark root cellar with his weapon at the ready.

Chase quickly followed, easing the door back into place as quietly as possible. The clank of the metal latch settling into place reverberated through him and ratcheted up his tension.

Sudden light from Alex's flashlight dispelled the total blackness and revealed the rows of canned goods, baskets of vegetables and the incline ramp Chase had built for Lucinda, which led into the basement via a wooden door.

Calming his breathing, Chase retook the lead and opened the basement door. He swept the large space, determining it was clear, before stepping inside with Alex on his six. Another homemade ramp would take them into the kitchen. He and Alex positioned themselves on either side of the door, preparing to breach the house, when Chase heard Ashley's voice in his head. Or rather his headset.

"Sheriff, tell them to send Lucinda out and I'll go in."

Ashley's raised voice sent fear sliding through Chase. "No," he ground out as softly as he could, but loud enough for the sheriff to hear.

"Miss Willis, you are to stay back." Frustration vibrated through the sheriff's voice. "I will put you in handcuffs if I have to."

Forcing himself to stay focused on the job at hand and not on Ashley's stubborn refusal to keep herself safe, Chase turned the knob and slowly opened the door. Alex moved past him, turning to the left while Chase entered to the right. The kitchen was clear.

From the other side of the wall separating the kitchen from the living room, Chase heard Lucinda's soothing tone.

"Are you sure you want to do this?" Lucinda asked. "Why ruin your lives when you don't even know why you're here?"

Chase had to smile. Leave it to Lucinda to pull out the men's story.

"Listen, lady, the boss gave us a job to do and we have to do it or—" The man's voice shook with agitation and sounded familiar to Chase.

"Shut up!" a second man barked out the command.

This man's voice also rang a bell. These were the same thugs who had found them at the cabin.

Where was the third man? Probably watching the sheriff's station.

Alex and Chase stacked up at the edge of the wall. With a quick tap on the shoulder from Alex, Chase and Alex stormed into the living room, Chase going to the left and Alex to the right. Two men stood on either side of the front plate glass window. The one on the left held a semiautomatic pistol while the other had a Glock, similar to what Chase used, tucked into his waistband. Lucinda was in her wheelchair in the middle of the living room.

"Hands in the air," Chase yelled.

"Drop your weapons," Alex shouted.

Surprise marched across both men's faces. The man closest to Alex held his hands up.

Alex rushed forward and disarmed the man and cuffed him.

Chase advanced on the other guy holding a weapon. "Set it on the ground."

Slowly, the man complied, putting the pistol on the rug at his feet.

Chase rushed forward and kicked the gun aside. "Turn around."

For a moment the guy hesitated, then finally turned. Chase holstered his weapon and took out his cuffs, slapping them around the guy's wrists. Once he had the man secured, Chase knelt beside Lucinda, visibly searching for signs of abuse. "Are you okay? Did they hurt you?"

"I'm not hurt," she replied.

Hanging his head with overwhelming relief, Chase sent up praise to God for the blessing.

"Suspects secure," Alex said into his headset.

"Chase." The urgency in Lucinda's tone brought Chase's gaze up.

"There's another one. In the—"

A loud crash reverberated through the house.

"What in the world?" Alex exclaimed.

A black SUV broke through the garage door and shot out onto the street, tires squealing.

Through the front window, Chase watched

the sheriff jump out of the way as the SUV sped onto the street, barely missing the sheriff's vehicle. Then a streak of green roared past. Nick Delaney's Humvee rammed into the getaway vehicle, sending the Escalade sliding into a telephone pole. A flash of blond hair in the back seat sent Chase's stomach plummeting. Ashley was in the Humvee.

Both automobiles came to an abrupt halt.

Fear galvanized Chase into action. "You got these two?"

"Yes," Alex replied. "Go."

Running out the front door, Chase couldn't help the litany of words streaming from his mouth. "Please, Lord, don't let her be hurt." Chase couldn't bear the thought he'd let Ashley down…again.

ELEVEN

As Nick rammed his vehicle into the escaping black SUV, the inside of the Humvee rattled from the vibration of the impact and shuddered through Ashley. The echo of metal colliding, twisting and bending as the two vehicles locked in a forceful battle rang in her ears.

Thankfully, the seat belt strap pulled tight, locking her in place in the middle of the back seat. She would probably have a bruise from the wide piece of heavy fabric, but that was such a minor thing, considering all she'd been through in the past few days. Her muscles already protested after bracing herself for the crash and made any movement painful as she shifted on the seat, trying to see out the front window.

Now that the black SUV was pushed up against a telephone pole, metal falling off it and steam rising from the engine, the rush of adrenaline ebbed but did little to ease the flutters in her tummy or slow her heart rate.

From what Ashley could discern, the Humvee had sustained minimal damage.

In the front seat Nick fought with the air bag, pushing it out of the way. Then he unclipped his seat belt and turned around to face her. "Are you okay?"

"I'm good. What about you? Did the air bag hurt you?"

He grinned, his dark eyes dancing. "Nope. You were right to have me push the front seat back as far as it would go. The air bag barely touched me when it deployed. And the seat belt kept me from flying out the window." He touched his chest. "I'll be sore, but it was worth it."

"We got him!" Jubilantly, she held up her hand for a high five and winced with the movement. Her whole body contracted and protested. She needed more pain relievers and some ice packs.

Nick slapped his hand against hers. "It was quick thinking on your part."

She dismissed his praise with a smile. When she'd seen that SUV smash through Chase's garage door and zoom past the sheriff, clearly intending to escape, all she could think about was stopping the men inside. And the only way to do that was for Nick to hit the gas and ram into the other vehicle.

Just then the door to the back passenger seat opened with a jerk and Chase ducked his head inside, his wide-eyed gaze frightened. "Ashley! Are you hurt?"

She unbuckled the seat belt and slid carefully toward him along the bench seat. "I'm fine. We're fine. But we got them."

"Him," Chase corrected. "There was only one person in the vehicle."

Through the front windshield, Ashley watched Daniel checking on the occupant of the SUV. A distant siren heralded the approaching ambulance.

Chase turned his stormy gaze to Nick. "That was reckless and stupid. You both could've been killed. What were you thinking?"

Quickly, Ashley held up a hand, keeping Nick from talking. "This was my idea. I had to do something to help. I'm tired of sitting on the sidelines, watching everybody else do the work, while I cower in the corner. If I could've driven this Humvee by myself, I would've." She cast Nick a glance. "But he wouldn't let me take over the wheel."

Nick held up his hands. "Hey, she's a force

to be reckoned with. You have your hands full, buddy."

Chase's jaw firmed. "Yes, I'm getting that idea."

Heat flushed through Ashley and she was sure her cheeks were bright red. "I'm right here." She gripped Chase's forearm. "Lucinda? Is she—" Ashley's breath laid trapped in her lungs as she waited to hear his answer.

"Unharmed," he said.

A swoosh of relief overwhelmed Ashley. She sank against the backrest and released her hold on Chase. "Thank you, Jesus."

Movement over Chase's shoulder drew her attention. Alex and the sheriff led two hand-cuffed men toward the sheriff's vehicle. Behind them, Lucinda wheeled herself out of the house, confirming Chase's words that the older woman was safe.

Focusing on Chase, Ashley placed her hand on his chest. His gear masked his heartbeat beneath her palm, but she could see the rapid pulse thumping at the base of his neck where his collar and the vest revealed his skin. He was still hyped from the situation. "I'm sorry that you were scared. But we're fine. Everything worked out."

"This time." He covered her hand with his.

"You can't do stuff like that. You have to stop trying to control everything."

His words pierced through her to the core. She did have an issue with control. How did she change that aspect of her personality?

Then he drew her out of the vehicle and into his embrace, his strong arms holding her close. Her arms went around his waist and she rested her head against his shoulder. She didn't want to ever leave the warmth of his hug. She wanted to snuggle closer, only there was all this stuff between them. Not only his tactical gear, but the specter of Maksim Sokolov and her imminent departure with the US Marshals into the WITSEC program.

"Nick Delaney!" Kaitlyn's strong voice rang out as the deputy marched toward the Humvee. "That was the most reckless, juvenile, thoughtless, inconsiderate and inconceivable thing I have ever seen anyone do! You could have been seriously injured."

Guilt for putting Nick in Kaitlyn's crosshairs blossomed in Ashley. She disengaged from Chase and hustled around to the other side of the Humvee to take responsibility, but this time it was Nick who held up a hand, staying her words.

He stood at the open door of the vehicle with

a wide grin as he faced the female deputy glaring at him. "Deputy Lanz, I didn't know you cared."

Chase's chuckle drew Ashley's attention. He'd followed her around the Humvee and now stood at her elbow. He leaned close to say, "I'm sure Lucinda would like to see you."

Knowing he was right and that neither Nick or Kaitlyn needed them gawking as they verbally sparred, Ashley tucked her arm through Chase's and hurried to Lucinda's side. The older woman spread her arms wide, inviting Ashley in for an embrace.

Ashley bent forward to hug the older woman. Clung to her, really. Tears of gratitude that she was safe and sound stung Ashley's eyes. She finally released her hold on Lucinda and stared into her dark eyes. "I'm so sorry this happened. You should never have been in danger. This is all my fault."

Lucinda shook her head and waved a hand. "Not your fault, Ashley. Those men didn't know who they were dealing with." She beamed at Chase, obviously proud of the man she'd help raise. "And they are as scared of Mr. Sokolov as you are."

"Did they tell you that?" Chase asked.

Lucinda shielded her eyes against the April

sun to stare up at him. "They didn't have to. Anytime his name was brought up, the two men cringed. Whatever hold he has on them, it's strong."

Chase rubbed a hand over his jaw. "I kind of figured as much." He glanced around. "I don't want to take any chances that there are more of them lurking about." He grasped the handles of Lucinda's wheelchair. "Let's get you both inside."

A shiver of apprehension traipsed down Ashley's spine as she hurried to open the front door. Once they were inside the house, the adrenaline that had pumped through Ashley's veins ebbed and tremors worked over her flesh.

Chase locked the wheels on Lucinda's wheelchair and rushed to Ashley. Rubbing her arms, he said, "You've had a shock." He led her to the couch.

Appreciating his kindness, Ashley held his hand before taking a seat.

He gave her hand a squeeze before saying, "I need to talk to the sheriff to see if I can buy us some time before we have to go to the courthouse."

"That would be helpful," she said. "I'm

all sweaty and hot and I would really like to change my clothes."

"Same here." He left through the front door.

"Can I get you some water?" Lucinda asked as she unlocked her wheels.

Distressed, Ashley jumped to her feet. "I should be the one asking you if you need water or anything at all. You're the one who was just held hostage."

Without waiting for a response, Ashley rushed into the kitchen. She stopped as tears sprung to her eyes. Gripping the sink, she hung her head as the stress of the past few days washed over her. She'd never experienced such heaviness of heart. She'd put good people in jeopardy. Today could have ended so differently. Lucinda could have been seriously hurt or worse. Chase could have lost so much. But it would be over soon. They would be free of her and the danger she'd brought to this town and its citizens.

"Glasses are in the cupboard to the left of the sink on the bottom," Lucinda said from the threshold to the kitchen.

Ashley jerked upright and nodded with a forced smile. She grabbed two short water glasses and filled them with water from the refrigerator filter system. She handed one to

Lucinda. Her hands shook, and she sloshed water onto Lucinda's slacks.

Grimacing, Ashley set her glass down and grabbed a towel to wipe up the mess. "I'm so sorry."

Lucinda waved her away. "It's only water. It'll dry." She wheeled herself over the threshold of the kitchen and moved farther into the living room. "Come on, let's take our glasses and get you back to the couch. You're going to collapse if we don't."

The thought of collapsing actually sounded good to Ashley. Unsteady on her feet, she followed Lucinda back to the living room and sat down. Placing her glass on the coffee table, Lucinda wheeled closer and took Ashley's free hand. "Honey, what are you going to do about Chase?"

Ashley tucked in her chin, her eyes widening at the question. "Do about Chase?"

Belatedly, Ashley remembered the first time she'd been here and Chase had commented about Lucinda playing matchmaker. Ashley couldn't let this woman hope for something that could never happen. "There's nothing between Chase and me."

Lucinda patted her hand. "I don't believe that for a second and neither do you. I've known that boy his whole life. He was upset that I was in danger, but it was nothing compared to the anguish I saw on his face when he thought you might be hurt. My boy loves you. He may be too stubborn to realize it yet, though, so you're going to have to point it out to him."

Ashley's heart jumped into her throat. She set her glass down and retracted her hand from Lucinda. "No, no, no." Standing, Ashley paced back and forth in front of the couch, agitation running rampant through her body. "That can't be true."

"What do you feel for him, Ashley?"

Lucinda's softly asked question stopped Ashley in her tracks. If she was going to be honest with Lucinda, and with herself, she would admit that she had deep feelings for Chase. Feelings that she had no business having for him. Feelings that she had locked away and couldn't let out of the little cage she'd locked them in. Because if she admitted how much she cared for—maybe even loved—Chase, leaving him would only be that much more painful.

She faced Lucinda. "As soon as I give my deposition, I will be leaving with the US Marshals Service. I will never see Chase, or any of you, again."

Lucinda made a face and waved her hand, a gesture that was so innate to the older woman, Ashley fought a smile. "We can get around all that. What I want to know, Ashley, is are you willing to take the risk on Chase?"

Risk? The word reverberated through Ashley's brain. "I can't risk that something will happen to Chase, or you, again. My being here, in your lives, puts everyone at risk."

Lucinda's expression softened and her voice gentled. "Honey, there are no guarantees in life. God never said life would be fair, only that He would be with us in every circumstance."

Those words echoed inside of Ashley. Words she'd heard before and words she clung to now. "Though I agree with you that there are no guarantees, there are some things I can control. My leaving is one of those. I will not, in any way, shape or form, destroy Chase's life by staying here."

"He could go with you, you know." Lucinda's steady gaze pinned her to the floor. "That happens with witnesses. My husband was a police officer. I know how the witness protection program works. Family members can go with the witness."

Ashley's heart twisted in her chest. "Please, understand. He's not my family. He's yours."

All this talk of family and love was giving her palpitations. Her heart acted like the injured bird she'd once rescued and transported in a cardboard box to the bird sanctuary. Tap, tap, tap. Scratch, scratch, scratch. If her ribs weren't already sore from the seat belt, she'd guess they'd have been sore from the pain within her chest.

The door opened and Kaitlyn walked in. She leveled Ashley with a stern scowl. "Chase tells me it was your idea to ram the Humvee into the SUV."

"And what a good idea it was," Lucinda said.

Though Ashley was grateful to the older woman for her support, she faced Kaitlyn's displeasure head on. "Yes, it was my idea. I had to do something"

Kaitlyn harrumphed. "Well, he didn't have to go along with it. He was in the driver's seat."

Ashley grimaced. "To be fair, I told him if he didn't do it, I would push him out and drive the Humvee myself."

Kaitlyn's gaze narrowed. "And you would've too, right?"

Squaring her shoulders, Ashley said, "Yes. I've learned a lot from you and Chase and Leslie. I'm not going to be some idle victim any-more. I want to take control of my life. The first thing I need to do is tell my story to the DA and then—" Ashley's voice faltered as her determination tripped over itself. Taking a deep breath, she continued, "Then I'm going into witness protection. I am going to blossom. Because if I don't, then Mr. Sokolov has won even if he hasn't eliminated me as he'd like to."

The respect and admiration in Kaitlyn's eyes warmed Ashley's heart. "Good for you. I still think it was foolhardy to risk your life, and Nick's life, but I understand."

Ashley was certain Kaitlyn did. Because Ashley was pretty sure Kaitlyn would've made the same choice.

Chase stepped inside, his gaze meeting Ashley's. "You're right, Ashley, you do need to blossom."

Apparently he'd overheard her speech. Embarrassment heated her cheeks, but she refrained from putting her hands to her face or dropping her gaze. She meant what she'd said.

"And I will do everything in my power to make sure you can," he continued.

Ashley frowned, not sure what he meant and too afraid to ask. Then she mentally scoffed. She'd just told everybody she was going to take control of her life and stop being a victim. And yet she was too afraid to ask a simple question for clarification from Chase.

But with everybody staring at her, them—Lucinda's gaze was hopeful while Kaitlyn's was intrigued—Ashley decided the better course of action was to remain silent.

There was something in Chase's gaze that she couldn't decipher, something between respect and affection and fear. She wished they were alone so she could explore what was going on, what he was thinking. But then again, did she really want to open herself up to that kind of heartache?

"So, what's the plan now?" Ashley asked, needing to change the subject and direct the conversation toward actions rather than emotions.

"Kaitlyn's going to take you to Leslie's, while the sheriff and Alex process these guys. Daniel went with the injured man to the hospital and will make sure he doesn't escape."

"And you?" Ashley asked.

"I'm going to get Lucinda somewhere safe," he said. "Then I'll join you at Leslie's."

That was good news to Ashley. She didn't like leaving knowing Lucinda could still be in danger. Ashley went to Lucinda and kissed her cheek and whispered in her ear, "I'm sorry. I'm just not brave enough."

Ashley walked out, following Kaitlyn to her car. The second she settled on the passenger seat, she tilted her head back and closed her eyes. Silently she prayed, *Lord, give me strength.* Why did life have to be so hard?

Once the door closed behind Ashley and Kaitlyn, Chase stood there for a moment, his head bowed as he murmured a quick prayer, "Lord, please watch over Ashley."

He had to trust that Kaitlyn and Leslie would take care of Ashley until he could get there. But his next order of business was to ensure Lucinda's safety. He turned to his former nanny. "You need to pack a bag. I'm taking you out to the Johnsons' house. They've agreed to have you stay with them until this whole mess is over."

"That's awfully nice," she said. "I like them." She started to wheel away and then spun back toward him. "So, Ashley?"

Confused by her question because he'd already explained that she was going to Leslie's and then to the courthouse, he said, "I'm going to make sure she gets to the courthouse safely so she can give her deposition. Then I will wait with her until the US Marshals take her into protective custody." And he was going to make sure the marshals understood that if anything happened to her under their watch, they would have to answer to him, and all of Bristle Township.

"That's not what I meant." The intensity in her eyes made him twitchy. "I meant, what are you going to do about how you much you care about her?"

The question tied his stomach up in knots. He undid the straps on his flak vest. He had no idea what he was going to do about the emotions crowding his chest, emotions that all centered on one platinum blonde with big beautiful eyes. "I don't know what you're talking about."

"Seriously, you're going with that answer?" Lucinda wheeled herself to his side and leveled her arthritic index finger at him. "Chase Fredrick, I have known you your whole life. You have strong feelings for that young lady. And she has strong feelings for you."

Her pronouncement stilled his hands. He glanced at Lucinda and, noting the determined expression in her eyes, his stomach slid toward his toes. "Don't go getting any hopeful ideas about me settling down. I've already explained this to you. I like my life the way it is."

That the future stretched out in a lonely abyss before him was something he didn't want to address. "Ashley's leaving, so whatever emotion she, or I, feel toward one another stems from the circumstances. There's nothing lasting between us. I need to stay rational and keep my feelings out of this situation."

"You can't tell me that work is going to be the one and only thing in your life."

How many times had he heard this lecture? She sounded like a broken record. Only for some reason, her words stung now, where in the past he could laugh them off. He shrugged off his flak vest and set it on the couch before taking a seat to undo the laces on his boots. "Please, go pack your bag."

She hesitated for a moment and he thought she would continue her interrogation. But instead she whirled away and rolled down the hall to her bedroom.

Letting out a beleaguered sigh, Chase ran a hand over his stubbled jaw. He did have deep emotions for Ashley. Some of which he was afraid to label, but they were so muddled with fear and responsibility and protection, he didn't know which end of his emotions was up and which was down. But he'd told Lucinda the truth. He liked his life and he didn't want to make any changes. Or at least, that's what he told himself. And he used to believe it, 100 percent. But now…he couldn't deny the ache filling him, making him long to find a way to make a future with Ashley.

You could go with her.

The unbidden thought marched into his consciousness. That idea grabbed hold of his imagination and wouldn't let go. What would it be like to start over, a fresh and new life with Ashley by his side?

But he couldn't leave Lucinda behind. And he couldn't ask her to go. Plus, he would miss the community of Bristle Township, his co-workers, his friends and his church. He'd made a life for himself here. One apart from his parents, where no one wanted to use him as a way to gain access to the vaunted Fredricks.

Was he willing to give up his carefully constructed life for Ashley?

The answer should have come easily, but he was so conflicted. A state of being he didn't usually find himself in.

Frustrated, he marched into the bathroom and quickly showered and shaved, then changed into a fresh uniform. When he returned to the living room, Lucinda was waiting.

"Okay, this is the last thing I'm going to say on the subject," she said over her shoulder as she wheeled toward the front door. At the portal, she faced him, her earnest expression tearing his conscience. "Your job is not enough. You're going to grow old alone. You need Ashley and she needs you. Do what you have to do to be with her." With that, she opened the door and wheeled out, leaving Chase staring after her.

Shaking his head in a mix of exasperation and admiration, he hurried out and helped her into his truck, which thankfully the town's tow truck operator had dropped off while Chase was in the shower.

He started up the engine, but before throwing the gear into Reverse, he turned to Lucinda. "And this is going to be my last word on the subject. I love you and I need you to stay out of my business."

TWELVE

Ashley took a refreshing shower and then donned a change of clothes—black pants and a red cardigan over a white blouse. She'd stuffed all of her belongings into her duffel bag and took a moment to pray, thanking God for His provision and asking for His continued blessing and protection.

Once she'd done a second sweep of Leslie's bedroom to make sure she hadn't left anything behind, Ashley walked out to the living room to find Kaitlyn and Leslie deep in a hushed conversation. The two women stopped talking as soon as they noticed her.

For a moment, Ashley questioned if they'd been talking about her. She smoothed a hand over her hair, noting that it had grown and needed another trim. Or maybe she'd let it grow out. And she'd definitely change the color. She was so done with the platinum.

Shaking off the self-conscious doubt, she reminded herself she was leaving and after today these kind and thoughtful women would be out of her life.

Every cell in Ashley's body ached with sorrow and regret, knowing she was going to be walking out the door of Leslie's little cottage for the last time. She set her bags down and then impulsively hugged Leslie and Kaitlyn. They hugged her back. She struggled not to cry.

"I'm going to miss you both." Ashley's voice shook with suppressed tears. "I know we won't be able to stay in touch, but I will be praying for you both."

Leslie took Ashley's hand. "I wish there was something we could do. We are going to miss you, too"

Kaitlyn squared her shoulders and blinked rapidly. "You're going to do fine. You are strong and you're a survivor."

Though Kaitlyn had said those words before, Ashley still struggled to believe them. But she smiled at the female deputy, knowing Kaitlyn was determined not to show any weakness. "Thank you, Kaitlyn. You and Chase have taught me a lot about who I am and who I want to be."

"Chase is the one I'm going to be worried about when you leave," Leslie said. "He has it bad for you."

Frustration welled within Ashley. She didn't need to hear this again. Lucinda had said the same and more. But there was nothing Ashley could do about how Chase felt about her, or how she felt about him. The situation was what it was. She was leaving. She couldn't dwell on what would never be. She only could look forward, knowing that she had to be as strong as Kaitlyn believed her to be in order to survive.

Picking up her bag, Ashley briskly said, "It's time we leave for the courthouse. I'm sure that the Los Angeles district attorney is getting antsy. I just want to get this all over with."

Kaitlyn moved to the window and looked out. "We have a few more minutes to wait."

"What do you mean?" Ashley asked.

Kaitlyn turned from the window. There was a mix of mischief and sadness in her eyes. "Chase wants to take you to the courthouse. I'm going to follow to make sure you make it there safely."

Ashley's stomach knotted. Though she would be seeing Chase again at the courthouse, she hadn't expected to be in close quarters with him. How was she going to make the trek from

Leslie's ranch to town with Chase and keep from saying something she might regret?

Something like, I love you and I can't live without you. The thought rocked her back a step. Did she love Chase? As in forever and ever. The answer danced at the edge of her mind and she quickly tamped down the tender emotion. Love had no place in her life. She had to do the right thing. Leave with no strings tied to Chase or anyone else.

Her throat grew tight. She forced out what she wanted to say. "Can't you just take me?"

Kaitlyn's smile was gentle. "You need this time with Chase. He needs this time with you. I'm not going to ruin it for him, or for you."

The sound of tires on the gravel drive announced Chase's arrival.

"Here he is," Kaitlyn said as she opened the door.

Ashley hesitated, bracing herself and shoring up her defenses. No matter what her emotions were, no matter how hard it would be to say goodbye to Chase, she had to. She had to keep her emotions in check.

Leslie put her hand on her shoulder. "Be of good cheer. For the Lord is with you and He will guide you wherever you go."

Ashley pressed her lips together for a moment to keep a chuckle at bay. "I think you're blending a couple of Bible verses."

Leslie grinned. "I'm sure I am. Memorizing Scripture was never my strong suit. But it sounds good and I do believe it."

Ashley quickly hugged Leslie with her free arm. "Thank you again."

Lifting her chin and straightening her spine, Ashley walked out of the cottage. Chase climbed out from the cab of his truck. He looked so good in a fresh uniform, his sandy blond hair still slightly damp and his jaw clean-shaven. She swallowed the lump in her throat along with the urge to run into his arms. On stiff legs, she walked forward as he jogged to the passenger side and opened the door for her. He took her bag from her hands, their fingers brushing briefly. Little zips of sensation tingled up her arm and settled near her heart.

She climbed into the truck and buckled the seat belt with shaky hands. If only things were different…she slammed the door on any thoughts that would lead her down the road to heartache. Folding her hands in her lap, she stared straight ahead.

Chase conversed with Kaitlyn before he climbed back inside the truck and drove away from the Quinn ranch. Once they were on the road headed back toward town, she glanced in the side-view mirror to see that Kaitlyn was, indeed, following close behind them.

The silence was thick in the cab of the truck. Ashley searched for something to say, for some inane topic to discuss to relieve the choking sensation of the air being sucked out of her lungs. But she came up empty.

So she settled for embracing the tension. She should have been used to this by now. Her whole life had been about dealing with one crisis and the next. Living with her mother had taught her how to cope, and going on the run had driven the lesson home.

Now, she was going to be joining the ranks of the many unnamed witnesses who disappeared from their everyday lives, reborn with a new name.

As they neared the courthouse, Chase eased up on the gas. "This isn't a good sign."

On the courthouse steps, a group had gathered. A TV news van from Denver was parked at the curb. Ashley spotted Lucca Chin with his notepad and pen. Her stomach sank. The last thing she needed was her face plastered all over the media.

Chase took a sharp turn down an alley and pulled around to the back of the courthouse to park. She could always count on him to know what to do.

He popped open his door, but Ashley put a hand on his arm. "Chase."

"Ashley?" He pulled the door closed and turned to face her, his eyes troubled. The longing in his tone had her heart pounding in her chest.

She tried to fill her gaze with all the love and affection she harbored for this man, because she could never say the words.

With her right hand, she unbuckled her seat belt while she fisted her left hand in his shirt. This was their one and only opportunity before she disappeared again. She leaned forward, hoping, praying he would close the distance because she needed this kiss. Something she'd been longing for from the moment she'd first laid eyes on Chase Fredrick.

Just one kiss to keep in her memories for the rest of her lonely life.

Chase's breath caught in his throat. There was no mistaking the invitation Ashley was extending. His rational brain said, *No, don't do it.* Giving in to the yearning to press his lips to this woman's would end up hurting them both.

But at the moment he didn't want to be rational, he didn't want to do the right thing by denying her something they both apparently wanted.

He wanted to kiss this woman more than he wanted to draw his next breath.

Closing the distance between them, he sealed his mouth over hers. Her lips were soft and pliable. He cupped the back of her head and deepened the kiss. Her right hand gripped his biceps while her left hand relaxed and splayed open across his chest. The heat of her palm burned through to his heart. No doubt she could feel the thunder of his heartbeat. He was surprised she couldn't hear the roar of his pulse. He certainly did.

When the kiss gentled and slowly ended, they drew apart and he dropped his forehead to hers. They were both breathing hard, their breaths mingled, fogging the windows despite the warmth of the spring sun outside. He searched for something to say that wouldn't shatter the moment, that wouldn't destroy the connection binding him to her. He remained silent, just breathing in her scent of vanilla and lavender and woman. He never wanted to leave the truck. How was he going to say goodbye?

Finally, she drew back. Her eyes misted. "Thank you."

He chuckled, his ego puffing up. "For the kiss?"

She gave him a soft, sweet smile that wrapped around his heart like a big red bow. "For the kiss. For everything. I wouldn't be alive if it weren't for you. I just want you to know how very grateful I am and how very much I will miss you."

His heart ached at the bittersweet melancholy that filled him. He reached for her, hoping to ease the pain in his chest. "I'm going to miss you, too."

She scooted back, out of his reach, pressing against the door. Her hand groped for the door release. "We need to go."

He hated hearing the sound of choking despair in her voice. This was hard for her. This was hard for him.

But she was right; they had to leave the confines of the truck and face what waited inside the courthouse. He gathered his rational side and wrapped it around him like an invisible cloak of sanity. He gave a sharp nod and opened his door. "Sit tight."

He climbed out, jogged around to her side and opened the door, his gaze searching the area to make sure there was no one in the vicinity who posed a threat.

He grabbed her bag and placed his hand at the small of her back, then guided her through the back entrance of the courthouse, past the restrooms and the court records room. They hurried to the main lobby. He could hear the clamoring outside the main doors. The media wanted in. A security guard Chase didn't recognize manned the door, keeping the news reporters from entering the building.

Taking a breath, Chase gestured toward Donald Grayson, the lawyer who sat on a bench down the main hallway. "We should talk to your lawyer."

As Chase led Ashley forward, he couldn't ignore the niggling at the base of his neck.

Donald rose from the bench outside the courtroom and stalked toward them, looking very citylike in his double-breasted gray suit and red power tie.

"It's about time you got here," Grayson said. "The district attorney and his assistant are getting nervous."

"We're here now," Chase said.

Grayson's mouth firmed. "I can see that. I would like a moment with my client alone, if you don't mind, Deputy Fredrick."

Knowing he had no choice, Chase nodded and stepped a few feet away. Far enough to give them privacy, yet close enough that he could reach Ashley within seconds if needed. For as long as he could, he would protect her despite his heart bleeding and breaking with the knowledge that he was going to have to let her go.

"Hi, Deputy." Mrs. Hawkins, the town librarian, walked past. She was a stout woman with auburn hair wrapped into a twist on the top of her head.

"Ma'am," he said. "What brings you to the courthouse today?"

She handed him a flyer. "We're starting a book club and I dropped some flyers off in the records office."

He glanced at the paper in his hands and thought about Ashley's love of books. This was something she'd enjoy. Sadness thrummed in his veins.

"You might want to go out the back door," Chase told her. "There's a lot of people out the front door."

"I saw that." She peered at him with curiosity evident in her gaze through her red-framed glasses. "What's all the ruckus?"

Not about to explain Ashley's predicament, Chase said, "Do you know the new security guard?"

Mrs. Hawkins glanced to the front door. "He must be Jarvis's replacement. I know he was going to retire."

That made sense. Just because he didn't know the new hire didn't mean there was cause to panic.

Every month people moved to the small mountain haven of Bristle Township in search of a simpler life. A simpler life had been very alluring along with a job with the Sheriff's Department. He'd thought that he'd grow old here in Bristle Township, serving its citizens and keeping the town safe. But now he wasn't sure that staying was what he really wanted.

You could go with her.

But did she want him to?

Ashley could feel Chase's gaze on her. It took all her effort not to turn toward him and see his expression, to discern what he was thinking and feeling about her. About the kiss.

Her lips still tingled. She'd known that kissing him would leave an indelible mark on her, not a visible sign but an inner stamp that would forever remind her of him. But more than that was the knowledge that no matter where she went or what she did in this life, there would always be a part of her missing. A part of her staying here in Bristle Township with Chase.

"Miss Willis."

Ashley blinked, realizing that Mr. Grayson was talking to her and she hadn't heard a word. The grim set to the lawyer's mouth had her stomach knotting and her muscles bunching with tension. "Is something wrong?"

"I don't like this situation at all," he said. "I find it hard to believe that the district attorney's office of Los Angeles had a burglary. Sounds fishy to me."

She shrugged, knowing the truth did stink. "Maksim Sokolov has people everywhere."

"I do believe you're right," Mr. Grayson said. "From all accounts this man has managed to stay out of the law's reach for a long time. Hopefully, now his reign of terror and corruption will end soon. Mr. Nyburg seems determined to bring the man to justice."

She was glad to hear of his determination. It would take a strong and stalwart personality to go up against a man as powerful as Maksim Sokolov. She hoped the district attorney watched his back.

"Let's get to the business at hand. Remember the drill from the last time?"

As if she could forget. The last deposition had left her drained. She could only imagine how much worse it would be in person. "Yes, I do. Only answer the question that is asked of me with as little verbiage as possible."

"Correct." He drew her to the bench seat. He opened his briefcase on his lap and handed her a stack of papers. "This is the transcript from the last time. I want you to read it over so your answers match. You won't have that inside the court, but at least this will refresh your memory just in case."

She didn't think her memory needed to be refreshed. She could remember every last detail of the video deposition, but she did as Mr. Grayson asked and read through the transcript. "Is there a reason the transcript can't be used in place of an in-person deposition?"

Grayson made a face. "The defense attorney protested using the transcript or the sheriff's copy of your deposition, saying there was no way to verify that the documents hadn't been doctored."

Ashley swallowed back a nervous lump. "Is the defense attorney here?" She remembered the coldness in his eyes and the way he'd grilled her, making her feel small and unworthy.

Mr. Grayson splayed his hands across the top of his briefcase. "He is here. But you have nothing to worry about. Don't let him intimidate you. If he gets out of line, I will stop him."

She had no doubt that Mr. Grayson would have her back. Just like Chase. She glanced over to where he stood with his back against the wall and his gaze on her. She gave him a soft smile, which he returned. Her insides strained with regret and longing.

The doors to the courtroom opened and four people walked out and headed in their direction. Ashley recognized the district attorney and his assistant. The other two men were strangers. Mr. Grayson stood, urging Ashley to do the same by cupping her elbow.

"Miss Willis?" the bigger of the men asked.

Ashley nodded. Her tongue remained glued to the roof of her mouth beneath the man's scrutiny. She was aware that Chase had stepped to her side. She could only imagine that, from an observer's point of view, the three of them were facing off with the four strangers. For some reason the music from *West Side Story* played through her mind.

"US Marshal Dirk Grant," the big man

spoke. He had wide shoulders beneath his navy blue suit. He flashed a badge, then gestured to the other man, similarly dressed. "This is my partner, US Marshal Keenan Hawks. We will be taking you into our custody now."

District Attorney Nyburg stepped forward. "Not before she's disposed." He looked at Ashley, his gaze concerned. "You are ready, correct?"

Taking a fortifying breath, Ashley nodded. "Yes, sir, I'm ready."

"Good. We need your testimony to convict Sokolov of murder and put him away for life. Let's get this show on the road." Mr. Nyburg turned and hurried back inside the courtroom. His assistant hesitated, and then quickly followed her boss, her heels clicking on the linoleum floor.

"This way." Marshal Grant indicated for Ashley to step between him and Marshal Hawks. "We will escort you into the courtroom."

Every cell in Ashley's being rebelled. She didn't want to go inside the courtroom. She didn't want to become their responsibility. She didn't want to leave Chase. But she had to. She handed Mr. Grayson back his papers. She glanced up at Chase, wanting to say something but afraid that only a squeak would come out because her throat was closing with despair and anguish. His jaw was tight, his eyes turbulent. She gave him a nod and stepped between the two marshals.

"Wait." Chase stopped them.

Ashley turned to him, her heart pounding in her ears. She wanted to run into his arms and ask him to whisk her away. She stayed in place.

"I need a moment with Miss Willis," Chase said, his voice strained.

Marshal Grant sighed. "Deputy, she's in our custody now."

"This is personal," Chase said. "I need to talk to Ashley."

Desperate to have one last moment alone with him, Ashley looked at Marshall Grant. "Please," she managed to say, her voice barely making it past the constriction in her throat.

The two marshals exchanged a glance. Marshal Grant nodded.

"Two minutes," Marshal Hawkes said.

Ashley hurried to Chase. He wrapped an arm around her shoulders and led her out of earshot of the men watching them. She stared at him, memorizing every line and angle of his face.

Keeping their backs to the men, he met her gaze. "I will go with you."

His words caused confusion to tear through her veins. She couldn't have heard him right. "With me?"

He had to mean he would go into the courtroom with her. Right?

"Yes." He nodded as if affirming his decision. "I will go with you into witness protection."

Her heart fluttered in her chest. The world tilted on its axis. What was he saying? "Why would you do that? Your life is here. Lucinda is here."

A muscle ticked in his jaw. "I can't stand the thought of you being alone and unprotected."

She wanted to weep. It wasn't a declaration of love but she understood that he wasn't making this offer lightly. Lucinda's words replayed in her head, telling her that he loved her. And as much as she wanted to grab hold with both hands and say, *Yes, come with me*, she would not let him sacrifice his life for her. As much as it wounded her, she accepted what she had to do. "Chase, you and I are never going to work. This is just a momentary blip in the grand scheme of things."

He frowned. "Ashley, I—"

"No." She cut him off, knowing that if he said the words, she would not have the strength to deny him. And deny him she must. "I'm sorry. I can't risk my heart to anyone. Life is too precarious and I'm not willing to be hurt or to hurt anyone else. And that includes you." Then she sealed her own coffin by uttering the words, "I can't love you."

An agonizing cry of grief built inside her chest. Tears burned the backs of her eyes. If she didn't walk away now, she was going to embarrass them both by breaking down into a sobbing, quivering mess. She turned and ran for the restroom she'd seen on the way in.

"Miss Willis!" Marshal Grant's shout followed her.

Once inside she slumped against the wall and let the tears flow.

THIRTEEN

Chase watched Ashley dip into the women's restroom at the far end of the corridor. The two marshals hurried after her, stopping outside the door, their expressions frustrated as they banged on the door.

I can't love you. The words echoed through Chase's brain, knocking against his skull until he thought they might break free. His feet were rooted to the floor. He wasn't sure what to think. He'd thought she'd be happy for him to go with her. But evidently, he'd misread her feelings for him.

"What did you say to her?" Donald Grayson asked.

Rubbing his jaw, which was as sore as if he'd been punched, Chase said, "Obviously something she didn't want to hear."

The courtroom doors banged open again. The district attorney's assistant walked out.

She hitched her purse higher on her shoulder as she came over to them. "Excuse me? Where is our witness?"

Chase gestured down the corridor. "Restroom. She'll be out soon."

The woman's gaze narrowed, then she walked past them. She spoke briefly to the marshals. The two men didn't look happy, but they walked back to where Chase stood.

"Deputy, it would be better if you left the witness to our care," Marshal Grant stated.

Chase nodded but didn't move. He couldn't leave, not like this. He had to make sure Ashley was okay. He hadn't meant to upset her. He only wanted to make her happy and keep her safe.

Ashley had ignored the banging on the restroom door and Marshal Grant's demand that she come out at once and was glad when the noise finally ceased. She wasn't ready to face them. She wasn't ready to face anyone yet. She needed this moment to grieve, to let go of the foolish notion that she could somehow live a normal life, fall in love—who was she kidding, she did love Chase—and become part of the Bristle Township community.

There were voices outside the door, one of

them definitely female. A moment later, the door to the restroom opened and the Los Angeles district attorney's assistant, Sarah Miller, walked in, looking cool in her gray pencil skirt, white blouse and high heels. The brunette's green eyes assessed Ashley.

Self-consciously, Ashley pushed herself away from the wall and pulled herself together as best she could. She splashed water on her face, washing away the tears. However, nothing could wash away the anguish burrowing into her heart.

Sarah leaned against the counter, holding onto her purse strap. "I know this can be hard. You don't have to do this if you don't want to. You can back out."

Ashley doubted Mr. Nyburg would appreciate his assistant saying Ashley had a choice in testifying. "I want to tell my story. It's my duty. I have to do the right thing."

Sarah grimaced. She reached in her purse and pulled out her cell phone, quickly sending off a text. "I was afraid you were going to say that."

"What is that supposed to mean?" Ashley asked. She dried her hands with a paper towel and tossed it into the trash bin.

"We all have to do what we have to do,"

Sarah said. "Sometimes to protect ourselves, sometimes to protect those we love."

Ashley didn't understand the woman's cryptic remark. And she didn't have time for riddles. Straightening her shoulders, she headed for the door. "I'm ready to get my deposition over with."

Sarah pushed away from the counter and blocked her path. "Not just yet."

Ashley frowned, not liking the anxiety roaring to life within her gut. "What do you mean, not just yet?"

The shrill sound of the fire alarm going off jolted through Ashley. And then the ding of an incoming text punctuated the noise.

Sarah looked at the text message and then shoved her phone back in her purse. When she withdrew her hand, she held a small black gun and aimed the barrel at Ashley.

Stunned, Ashley stepped back, aware there was nowhere to run. "What are you doing?"

The woman's hard expression didn't bode well. "I'm sorry, Miss Willis. But you're going to come with me."

Was the woman working for Sokolov? Fear slid over Ashley's skin like sandpaper. "The marshals are right outside the door." As was

Chase and the courthouse security guard. What did this woman think she was going to do?

"Don't worry about them," Sarah said.

She gestured with the gun for Ashley to precede her to the door. As soon as she was behind Ashley, Sarah crammed the business end of her weapon into Ashley's ribs. Fear exploded inside Ashley. Her mind scrambled through the self-defense tactics that Chase had taught her. Kicks and jabs came to mind, but would she be quick enough or would Sarah pull the trigger before Ashley could get away?

Sarah said, "Open the door slowly."

Deciding to comply for now, Ashley was met with a face full of billowing smoke. Her eyes instantly watered and her nose stung as she coughed in a lungful of acrid smoke. Where were the marshals? She could hear voices shouting but couldn't see anything in the thick gray smoke.

Sarah coughed behind her but managed to say, "Make noise and I pull the trigger. Turn to your left."

Left was in the direction of the door out of the building. But Ashley needed to go right to find Chase. The gun pressed harder into her rib cage.

"Do it. No screaming," Sarah demanded.

"I'll shoot you where you stand if you so much as make a peep."

Ashley clamped her lips together and closed her eyes. She sent up a silent plea to God for help.

Letting Sarah get closer, Ashley spun while at the same time jabbing her elbow into Sarah, knocking the hand holding the gun away. Free, Ashley turned to escape but tripped over a body lying on the ground in front of the door. She went down hard on her hands and knees.

Hands grabbed her, lifting her off the floor and securing her in a strong grip. For a moment hope flared that Chase had found her in the smoke, but an arm slid around her throat, putting pressure on her trachea and disabusing her of the notion that her helper was friendly. She kicked and clawed at her captor.

She let out a scream that was cut off as something touched her side and sent an electric shock through her system. Her whole body stiffened as pain ricocheted through her muscles. The shock was only an instant but enough to make her body go limp with relief when it ended.

Her feet no longer touched the ground as the man holding her lifted her and tightened his arm around her neck, cutting off her air supply. She scratched at the arm, trying desperately to turn her head and wedge her chin into the crook of his elbow the way Kaitlyn had instructed but she was so weak from the electrical shock.

"Cooperate or I'll zap you again," a deep male voice said into her ear.

She stilled, her mind rebelling at suffering another jolt of electricity.

He released the pressure on her neck.

Her attacker set her feet on the floor and pushed her forward. "Move it."

Using the hem of her shirt as a filter against the thick gray smoke, Ashley couldn't see anything so she put her free hand out in front of her. She bumped up against the wall.

"Find the door," Sarah gasped from behind her between coughs.

Holding her breath, Ashley groped around. She found the hinge of the door. She finally had to breathe in. Her lungs hurt and she doubled forward to cough.

Her attacker shoved her hard into the door and the bar released upon impact. Ashley stumbled out into the fresh air with the man, who wore a face mask and was dressed as the courthouse security guard, and Sarah following her. The door slammed shut behind them.

Ashley breathed in deep, trying to clear the smoke from her lungs. She wiped at her watery eyes. They were at the back of the building. The fire alarm continued its cry and mingled with the sound of the fire engines arriving at the scene.

A big black car rolled up in front of them and the door opened. "Get in!" shouted a gruff voice.

A voice Ashley knew from her nightmares. She shrank back, looking for a way to escape.

"Go." The security guard shoved Ashley forward so that she had no choice but to climb into the back of the limousine. She settled on the seat and stared at the man who wanted to kill her. Sarah climbed in behind her, while the security guard joined the driver in the front seat.

Maksim Sokolov looked at her like she was gum stuck on the bottom of his shoe. "So you're what all this fuss is about."

He knocked on the window separating the back compartment from the driver, apparently giving the signal to go. The Lincoln Town Car drove away from the courthouse, dodging pedestrians and emergency equipment. Ashley twisted in her seat in time to see Chase and the marshals burst through the back entrance door. Chase ran after them but the speeding limo was too fast. Within moments, they were leaving downtown Bristle Township.

"I love you," Ashley whispered, convinced she would never see Chase again.

The moment the fire alarms sounded, Chase had known something was wrong. The billowing smoke was thick and hard to navigate. People poured out of the courtrooms and the court's records room. He'd raced to the restroom, urging people to move out of the way, only to find it empty and the marshals unconscious on the ground.

After making sure they were both alive, Chase ran for the back exit in time to see a black town car speeding away with Ashley in the back seat. Frantic, with fear freezing in his veins, he ran after the car but was no match for the moving vehicle.

Still running, he doubled back and jumped into his truck. As he started the engine, Marshal Grant jumped into the passenger seat. "I'm coming with you." He had a nasty knot forming on his head that no doubt hurt. "Hawks will follow in our vehicle."

"Shouldn't you be checked out by a paramedic?" Chase asked the question as he threw the gear into Drive. Before the man could buckle up, Chase stepped on the gas and drove in the direction the town car had taken.

"I'm fine," Grant said, bracing himself on the dashboard.

"Call for backup," Chase told the marshal. "Ashley's been taken. We have to stop them before they kill her."

The terrorizing thought robbed him of breath. He fought to maintain his cool and not give in to the rising panic.

At the intersection where he had the choice to turn right toward Denver or left toward the backside of Eagle Crest Mountain, Chase faltered and prayed for inspiration.

He thought about the private airstrip at the top of the mountain attached to the Eagle Crest Resort and the car service the resort provided for its guests. Chase was sure he recognized that limo as one used by the resort. He had to take a chance. He turned left, heading toward the mountain pass.

Beside him, Grant was talking to the sheriff.

"Put that on speaker, would you?" Chase said.

Grant complied. "Sheriff, I have you on speaker now with Deputy Fredrick."

"Sir," Chase said, "we're going up the mountain to the airstrip at the top."

"Playing a hunch?"

"Yes, sir." Chase tightened his grip on the steering wheel as he took the corners on the winding mountain road at top speed. "A man like Sokolov wouldn't go commercial."

"Agreed."

Stomach churning with anxiety, Chase said, "But in case I'm wrong, alert the state patrol to watch for a black limousine with the license number 359 XTL."

"Roger that." The sheriff's deep timbre filled the cab of the truck. "Marshal Hawks and Daniel are headed your way."

Marshall Grant clicked off and frowned at Chase. "I hope you're right about this. If we lose Miss Willis, it's your fault."

Chase didn't need that reminder. Guilt threaded through his system like the laces of his boots. He should've waited until after the deposition to talk to Ashley about joining her in WITSEC. Or better yet, he shouldn't have said anything at all.

Now that he grasped she didn't share the same emotions about him, he regretted letting down his defenses and opening himself up for rejection. Though he couldn't find it within himself to harbor any ill will for the woman who had captured his heart. His love was unconditional. And he would do everything in his power to ensure that the woman he loved lived to see that Maksim Sokolov rotted in prison.

Ashley noticed the terrain outside the speeding car's window. They were driving the same road that the fake Detective Peters had taken the day he'd forced her into his SUV. They were headed up the backside of the mountain. What was Mr. Sokolov's intention? To throw her off the cliff?

Her insides clenched with dread. She would fight to the end. She would not be easily disposed of. She hadn't come through this nightmare only to have it end like this.

But they passed the turnout spot where Chase had shot the fake detective and he'd been the one to go over the cliff. Was there another turnout they were heading for?

The car kept a steady pace, rounding the curves that hugged the mountain with a squeal of tires. The seat belt bit into Ashley's chest, poking at her already tender spots. Maksim Sokolov sat on the bench seat facing Ashley, his gaze never wavering.

He was older than she remembered, his skin

weathered and wrinkled. Up close like this, Ashley could tell the man had scars on his hands and one running down the length of his neck that disappeared beneath the collar of his black suit. She shivered with fear as she met his dark reptilian gaze.

Shifting her attention to the woman sitting beside her, Ashley asked, "Why are you a part of this ugliness?"

Sarah stared at her for a moment as if startled by the question. Her green eyes were anxious as the gun in her hand quivered. Her mouth moved but no words came out.

Maksim Sokolov sat forward to snatch the gun from Sarah's hand. "We don't want this to accidentally go off. That would be a mess to clean up."

He set the gun on the seat beside him.

Ashley focused on the weapon, her mind working out how to get her hands on it. Though she'd never fired a gun before, she figured simply pointing the weapon and squeezing the trigger would get the job done.

Maksim shook his finger at her. "Don't even think about it, young lady. I may be old, but I'm faster than you."

Ashley jerked her gaze back to his. "You should have just left me alone. I wasn't going to say anything to anyone until your assassin showed up."

He shrugged. "I couldn't take the chance that one day you'd grow a conscience."

A stab of guilt pricked her. She'd always had a conscience. She'd just been more afraid of him. And with good reason. But maybe if she'd come forward sooner on her own, Gregor would still be alive.

"Did you kill Gregor?" Her heart twisted with grief at the loss of her friend.

Maksim's lips thinned. "An unexpected casualty. But he'd outlived his usefulness, anyway."

Her fist clenched at his callous words. Gregor had been twice the man Sokolov was. "Did you set fire to the restaurant?"

He waved the question away as if swatting at a fly. "I no longer wanted the business," he said. "The insurance payout will allow me to open a new venture."

By burning down The Matador, he'd put people out of work and killed a man. Which she doubted bothered him at all. Talk about not having a conscience. "You're a horrible man," she said. Deciding she had nothing to lose, she asked, "Why did you kill Detective Peters?"

Maksim sneered, his face twisting in a way

that had Ashley's skin crawling. She pressed her back against the seat, wishing to put more distance between them.

"He betrayed me." Maksim nearly spit the words. "No one betrays me and lives."

"How did he betray you?" Ashley pressed. "He was a police officer doing his job."

"He may have been on the job but he was taking my payoffs until he decided to become greedy and wanted more," Maksim stated.

"So he was dirty," she murmured, disappointed that the officer had sold out his honor and integrity to Sokolov. What could have enticed Peters to turn against his oath to protect and serve? She guessed they'd never know.

"Everyone has dirt on their hands," Maksim said.

Once again Ashley turned her gaze to Sarah, who stared out the window with tears rolling down her cheeks. Reaching across the seat, Ashley gripped the other woman's hand.

Sarah startled, her head swiveling as her watery gaze met Ashley's.

"Tell me why you're doing this. Is it for money?"

Sarah shook off Ashley's hand. Her terrified gaze darted to Maksim before bouncing back to the side window. Sarah curled away from Ashley, keeping her hands out of Ashley's reach. Whatever hold Sokolov had on Sarah was strong. Ashley wasn't sure how to help her.

They finally reached the plateau at the top of the mountain. In the distance she could see Eagle Crest Resort. Ashley had never ventured to the resort but from what she could see of the large four-story structure with its peaked roofline, she understood the draw.

The hotel sat strategically on the tip of Eagle Crest Mountain and provided a panoramic view of the surrounding mountains. Though there was scant snow on the ground this late in April, there were people riding the lifts up and down the ski runs on the north side of the mountain. The other sides of the mountain were crisscrossed with hiking trails, which was a big draw for Bristle Township in the sunny months.

Why were they taking her to the resort?

The vehicle veered in an arc away from the main road leading to the resort and headed toward a private airstrip a football field length away from the main building. A small white jet with three round windows along its side stood on the tarmac. The jet's door was open and a set of stairs extended to the ground.

"Where are you taking me?" she asked.

Maksim's lips stretched in a smile that reminded Ashley of an evil clown. "Somewhere no one will ever find your remains."

Ashley's mouth dried at the blatant threat. She had to find a way to escape, but there was nowhere for her to go even if she managed to run off. She doubted she'd make it to the resort for help before they shot her. And taking off into the woods, well, the mountain had its own set of dangers.

The town car came to a halt. The driver jumped out and opened the back door, reaching inside to clamp a hard hand around her biceps. He yanked her out of the car. Maksim and Sarah followed.

Ashley had to do something to delay them. That is if Chase managed to figure out where she'd been taken. But she had no idea how he would know. She could only pray that God would give him the right knowledge.

Digging in her heels, she forced the driver to drag her. She wasn't going to make this easy for them. She kicked and punched at the behemoth man but her attempts to hurt him bounced off his hard muscles. She screamed at the top of her lungs, hoping somebody at the resort might hear.

Maksim smacked her across the face. Pain

exploded in her head and she tasted blood in her mouth. She lunged at him with her fists raised.

He darted out of the way. "This one's a wild-cat," he said. "When we get on the plane, re-strain her."

Sarah stopped walking. "What about me? We're square now, right? You'll let my son go?"

Ashley's heart sank. No wonder Sarah was helping him. Her child's life was in danger. Ashley asked the woman, "You destroyed the video deposition, didn't you?"

Sarah ignored her. "Please, Maksim, you promised me."

"Indeed, I did." Sokolov held the gun that Sarah had used to force Ashley from the court-house and aimed it at Sarah. "I'm done with you. You're nothing but a loose end."

There was no doubt about his intent. He was going to shoot Sarah. "You can't kill her," Ash-ley yelled. "She has a child. Don't you have any sense of decency in you?"

Maksim laughed. "No. Any sense of de-cency I had was beat out of me in prison years ago."

"There's no reason for you to harm her," Ashley pleaded. "Please, don't hurt her, too."

"You bleeding heart types," Maksim muttered and lowered the gun. "Get on the plane, both of you."

Maksim made a whirling gesture with his finger in the air. Ashley followed his gaze to where a man wearing a navy blue pilot's uniform appeared in the open doorway of the jet. The pilot disappeared and a few moments later the engine roared to life.

The man holding on to Ashley tugged her toward the jet. At the bottom of the staircase leading to the plane's door, Ashley grabbed the railing with her free hand and wrapped her legs around the bars. They were going to have to pry her loose and carry her up the stairs.

The squeal of tires on pavement rent the air. Chase's truck followed by a Sheriff's Department vehicle screeched to a stop a few feet away. Ashley nearly collapsed in gratitude. God had come through and sent Chase to the rescue.

Moving quicker than she deemed possible, Maksim rushed forward, pushing his man aside to grab Ashley. "Let go or I kill her." He aimed the weapon at Sarah.

Ashley released the stair railing. Maksim strong-armed her in front of him like a shield. Then he shot Sarah. Ashley screamed as the other woman crumpled to the ground. The driver and the pilot both disappeared inside the plane, leaving Maksim to fend for himself.

Maksim put the gun to Ashley's temple. "Climb the stairs. Those cops are going to have to go through you to get me."

Ashley could only pray that somebody would take the shot, regardless. Maksim Sokolov needed to be stopped.

Chase jumped out of the truck with his breath trapped in his lungs and his sidearm at the ready. Fear and anguish squeezed his insides at the gut-wrenching sight of Maksim Sokolov hiding behind Ashley. Her eyes were terrified and her face had lost all its color.

Holstering his weapon, Chase put his hands up and moved forward. "Mr. Sokolov, let's be reasonable here. There's no way you're getting off this mountain. If you harm her, you're going home in a body bag. I don't think you want that. You can run your operation from inside prison."

"I've been in prison," Maksim yelled back. "I'm not going back."

Marshal Hawks parked his vehicle in front of the plane, blocking the aircraft from leaving. Behind him Chase could hear Daniel saying he didn't have a clean shot.

Chase made a wide circle so that he wouldn't be in the pathway of the bullet when the opportunity for a shot presented itself.

Seeing that Maksim's finger wasn't on the trigger, Chase's gaze locked on to Ashley's. He couldn't let Maksim take her onto that plane. She would be as good as dead. He prayed that Ashley wasn't too freaked out. He needed her to keep her head and be focused.

"Now!" Chase shouted.

Without hesitation, she reacted. In one swift move, she cupped her fisted left hand with her right while jamming her elbow into Maksim's rib cage. At the same time she stomped on his instep.

The man let out a yowl of pain. She jerked out of his grasp but he grabbed her by the wrist before she could get away. She used the lessons in self-defense to lean into Maksim, swiftly yanking him off balance as she reversed her hold on his wrist and twisted his arm behind him.

Chase's breath caught and pride swelled.

But Maksim didn't go down as planned. He braced his legs apart, clearly understanding the move.

With a sickening laugh, Maksim cackled, "You think you're so smart." He brought the gun around and aimed the barrel at Ashley's face.

"Let her go," Chase yelled, even as he was running toward her.

Ashley released her hold on Makism. He tried to grab her again, but she dove to the side.

Three shots rang out as the two marshals and Daniel fired on Maksim, hitting him center mass. Blood blossomed in a widening crimson stain across his white shirt. Shock twisted his features as he went to his knees and then fell face first onto the tarmac.

Marshal Hawks and Daniel ran forward and entered the plane to apprehend the pilot and the driver.

Chase caught Ashley as she barreled into him. She clung to him and buried her face into his neck. Her body trembled within his embrace. "Shh. You're safe now. It's over."

She was finally free. She could resume her life, wherever she wanted it to be.

Chase longed to tell her that his love for her was real, that he would follow her to the ends of the earth. She only had to say the word. But he held back. He wanted her to have the choice.

She no longer had to live a life looking over her shoulder.

Daniel had Sokolov's two henchmen cuffed and sitting on the ground.

The two marshals stepped forward, taking Ashley from Chase. "We'll take our witness with us," Marshal Grant said.

"Chase?" The confusion in her eyes scored him.

"It's okay. You go with the marshals for now," he said. "Daniel and I will take care of this. You still need to give your deposition."

"But he's dead," she said. "He can't hurt me anymore."

Marshall Grant cleared his throat. "Maksim Sokolov may be gone, but until we take down his network, you need to stay in our custody."

Chase's stomach dropped. He should've thought of that. Would Maksim's men seek revenge against Ashley?

"But I don't know anything about the rest of his organization," Ashley said.

"We have another witness," Marshal Hawks stated. "You can give us the information we need in regard to Detective Peters's murder. Our other witness will provide the rest."

Chase frowned, wondering who this other person could be. But he wasn't given an opportunity to ask as sirens heralded the arrival of the ambulance and the squeal of more tires as Alex, Kaitlyn, the sheriff and the district attorney also arrived.

The sheriff stopped to talk to the marshals. Kaitlyn listened for a moment, then stalked toward Chase. Alex went to help Daniel with the two men. The district attorney rushed to Sarah's side and helped her to a seated position. One paramedic hustled to stop the bleeding in her shoulder, while the other checked Sokolov's body, then placed a white plastic sheet over his still form.

Ashley stood apart from everyone with her arms wrapped around her middle. She kept glancing toward Chase.

"Dude, really?" Kaitlyn walked up to him and punched him in the arm. "Are you going to let them take her away? You better fight for her! She loves you and you love her."

"Ouch!" Chase said, mostly to buy time as he processed her words. "She said she couldn't love me."

Kaitlyn slapped a hand to her forehead. "She didn't mean it. She doesn't want to make you choose her over your life here."

Chase's mind whirled. Did Ashley love him? Had she said she couldn't love him because she hadn't wanted to take him from his life in Bristle Township? He did love this town and the community, but he wanted to be with Ashley. And that was what he was going to do, if she'd have him.

He hurried to Ashley's side. Relief shone bright in her eyes as she gripped his hands.

Marshal Grant frowned. "What is it now, Deputy?"

"I need to tell Ashley something," Chase said.

"Again?" The marshal shook his head. "Last time didn't turn out so well."

Ignoring everyone else, Chase focused on Ashley. He squeezed her hands. "I know you said you can't love me. But I love you, Ashley Willis." He swallowed the lump of dread and apprehension forming in his throat. "And I want to spend my life cherishing you, protecting you and loving you."

Her eyes widened and a mix of doubt and joy filled her gaze. "Are you really willing to give everything up to be with me?"

"Yes," he said. "Whatever it takes."

Her eyes softened and she beamed at him. Joy spread over her lovely face. "When I told you I couldn't love you, that was a lie. My last one, I promise."

"So what is the truth?" he asked, his heart pounding with anticipation.

She cupped his face and looked deep into his eyes. "The truth is, Deputy Chase Fredrick, I love you. And I want to be with you, no matter what, no matter where."

Elated, he captured her mouth in a toe-curling kiss. He accepted and acknowledged that whatever the Lord had in store for them, for their future, they would face it together, forever.

EPILOGUE

Three months later

Overhead, lights danced in the night sky in a brilliant burst of colors. Ashley sat next to Chase on the park lawn in downtown Bristle Township. Lucinda sat in her wheelchair next to them with a blanket over her legs.

An unfamiliar warmth spread through Ashley as she contemplated the fact that Lucinda's matchmaking had come to fruition. However, Ashley believed God had brought her and Chase together. No other man could have breached the barricades of her heart. His innate kindness, loyalty and honor had drawn her to him, but his love had captured her heart. Soon they would marry and start a new life together. With children and love. Lucinda would one day get her wish of grandbabies to spoil.

All around them sat families and friends on

blankets or in chairs, as they watched the Eagle Crest Mountain Resort's Fourth of July lights show. "This is actually better than fireworks."

Chase tucked a chin-length strand of hair behind her ear. She'd gone back to her natural color of walnut brown and was letting it grow out.

"Every year is different," Chase said. "I enjoy the cartoon characters."

Ashley laughed. "I'm enjoying the flower display." A large rose blossoming held her interest.

"You're more beautiful than any flower," Chase murmured in her ear as he tightened his arm around her.

"Ashley?" a deep male voice asked.

Her heart skipped a beat. She recognized that voice. She'd never dreamed she'd hear it again. Ashley's gaze sought the man standing at the edge of their blanket. His hair was whiter than she remembered and his shoulders a bit more stooped. But it was him.

She gave a little gasp and jumped to her feet. "Gregor!"

After everything that had happened on the mountain, the marshals had finally revealed that they had faked Gregor Kominski's death to keep Maksim Sokolov from killing him. In return, Gregor had given them everything they needed to take down what remained of Sokolov's operation. Even though the mastermind behind the organization was dead, there'd been people who were loyal to him and who had expressed the need for revenge. The police had arrested them all.

The marshals had released both Ashley and Gregor from protective custody. They were given permission to go back to their lives with their own names. She, of course, returned to Chase and Bristle Township. Though she knew Gregor lived, she hadn't been able to see him and had no idea where Gregor had disappeared. But now he was here in Bristle Township. Her heart swelled with happiness.

His face and hands bore scars from the fire, but his eyes were still so kind. She hugged him tight. "I didn't think I'd ever see you again."

"I wasn't sure if you would want to see me," Gregor said, hugging her back.

"Of course I would," she exclaimed, choking back tears of gratitude. "You are a part of my life. An important part."

He leaned back to search her face. "I am glad. I never meant for you to be hurt."

She shook her head. "I wasn't, thanks to you."

Chase stood and shook the man's hand.

"Thank you for coming. And for all you did for Ashley."

Ashley turned to her fiancé. "You invited him here?"

Beaming, Chase slipped his arm around her waist. "I knew you would want to see him."

Love filled her to overflowing. Chase was the man she would marry and spend the rest of her days loving. And she couldn't be happier. "You are the best man in the whole wide world."

Chase laughed and introduced Gregor to Lucinda.

"Pull up a chair, young man," she said to Gregor. There was no mistaking the curiosity in Lucinda's eyes.

He smiled and seemed to stand taller. "Oh, I think I'm going to like you."

Chase somehow found a folding chair and put it next to Lucinda's wheelchair. Gregor sat and the two became fast friends.

Resuming their seats on the blanket, Ashley leaned back against Chase's chest and stared up at the beautiful display of lights in the sky.

She couldn't have asked for a better ending to her story.

But it wasn't an ending. It was the beginning. She looked at the diamond engagement ring sparkling on her finger, almost as bright as the lights overhead. The beginning of a new life with a new name—Mrs. Ashley Fredrick. She liked the sound of that.

* * * * *

*If you enjoyed this story,
look for* Buried Mountain Secrets, *Maya and Alex's story.*

Dear Reader,

I hope you enjoyed visiting Bristle Township, Colorado. Having the Rocky Mountains as the backdrop for this book and the previous one, *Buried Mountain Secrets*, is such a special treat. I love the mountains, the rocky terrain, the forest and the many ways that the setting plays a part in the story.

Ashley Willis found a safe haven when she landed in Bristle Township. But she felt guilt and shame for the secrets she kept. Pairing her with Deputy Chase Fredrick seemed like a good match for he was a man of honor and integrity, a man who would protect her and love her regardless of her past. And he needed someone who could love him for the man that he was, not for the family he came from. Together, they made a formidable team and won each other's hearts.

I hope to write more books set in Bristle Township, featuring the men and the women of the Sheriff's Department.

Until then, may God bless you and keep you in His care.

INTRODUCING OUR
FABULOUS NEW COVER LOOK!

COMING FEBRUARY 2020

**Find your favorite series in-store, online or
subscribe to the Reader Service!**

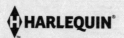

Get 4 FREE REWARDS!

We'll send you 2 FREE Books plus 2 FREE Mystery Gifts.

HEARTWARMING

Safe in His Arms

Anna J. Stewart

HEARTWARMING

The Rancher's Family

Barbara White Daille

Harlequin® Heartwarming™ Larger-Print books feature traditional values of home, family, community and—most of all—love.

FREE Value Over **$20**

THE FORTUNES OF TEXAS COLLECTION!

18 FREE BOOKS in all!

Treat yourself to the rich legacy of the Fortune and Mendoza clans in this remarkable 50-book collection. This collection is packed with cowboys, tycoons and Texas-sized romances!

YES! Please send me **The Fortunes of Texas Collection** in Larger Print. This collection begins with 3 FREE books and 2 FREE gifts in the first shipment. Along with my 3 free books, I'll also get the next 4 books from The Fortunes of Texas Collection, in LARGER PRINT, which I may either return and owe nothing, or keep for the low price of $5.24 U.S./$5.89 CDN each plus $2.99 for shipping and handling per shipment*. If I decide to continue, about once a month for 8 months I will get 6 or 7 more books but will only need to pay for 4. That means 2 or 3 books in every shipment will be FREE! If I decide to keep the entire collection, I'll have paid for only 32 books because 18 books are FREE! I understand that accepting the 3 free books and gifts places me under no obligation to buy anything. I can always return a shipment and cancel at any time. My free books and gifts are mine to keep no matter what I decide.

☐ 269 HCN 4622   ☐ 469 HCN 4622

Name (please print)

Address   Apt. #

City   State/Province   Zip/Postal Code

Mail to the Reader Service:
IN U.S.A.: P.O. Box 1341, Buffalo, N.Y. 14240-8531
IN CANADA: P.O. Box 603, Fort Erie, Ontario L2A 5X3